PERI

C.A. RICHARDS

*A **Leaves and Stars** Publication*

Printed in the United States of America

First Printing, 2015
Printed by CreateSpace

ISBN 978-0692469354

Leaves and Stars Publishing
8800 Stretch Lane
Bryan, TX 77808

To my mother and father
The first ones to believe

PART ONE
SPRING

I

Beginnings are tricky things. Just what is a beginning after all? The beginning of a story lies far before any book or account could record, for all events are related to all other events. If one goes back far enough one will eventually come to the point where all clear, concise thought is an illusion and thus impossible to attain. When is the beginning of a life or story? What about the ending? Are individual lives important, and if so can we truly separate each one to the individuality the single person possessed? And really, how can we know the truly correct answers?

Awake. Gasping for air. I open my eyes and blink a few times as they adjust to the low light surrounding me that feels like a direct spotlight.

Where am I?

It's misty and dark, and there seems to be a smell pervading the whole area. I realize I am sitting on the ground, and that this ground is moist with what feels like moss. I stand up to look around. I seem to be in some sort of walled in dead-end with rocky barriers on all sides. These walls form a square maybe ten feet wide on each side. I walk over to one of the walls to find a way out. Something is wrong, this is all wrong. Where am I? What is this place? And how could I have gotten here? Is there some purpose? I don't know.

I reach out to touch the wall in front of me, which seems strangely smooth. Suddenly I feel a burning sensation and retract my hand quickly, clutching it to my chest to subdue the apparent burns.

After a few moments the sensation fades away and I look at my hand to assess the damage. I bring my hand close to my face, only a few inches away, it's still so dark I can hardly see it.

The skin is clear, not a single burn, it's not even red. I notice a sort of light coming from my side in my peripheral and turn to look at the rocky wall, my mouth falls open. Where my hand pressed against the smooth stone of the wall there is a glowing blue handprint. I lean in closer and see details as minute as each swirl of my fingerprints, each gently glowing a bright blue coming directly out of the dark, rocky surface.

I back up a few steps from the wall, surprised and frightened by the glow. I back up too far and run into the opposite wall behind me, knocking my head against the hard rock. My back begins to burn and I spin around to see a rough outline of my body is now imprinted in blue against the wall. I back up again but this time remain careful to avoid the walls behind me, standing in the center of the enclosure.

Between the two glowing walls I stand and breathe heavily, the thick misty air not helping as I worriedly begin to realize that I still have not found any evident exits. I notice the ground is still moist and springy. I look down through the mist at what my feet are standing upon.

It looks similar to moss, but is a pale gray. It looks almost like rock itself though it's incredibly soft and seems to be holding water. I bend down to tentatively place my finger against the moss-rocks, and exhale a relieved sigh as neither a burning feeling nor a blue glow become evident. I press my hand a little into the springy substance and watch as water flows out onto my hand.

I press harder and the springy substance shifts over to make room for my hand, and giving me an idea. Plunging forth my hands I mold the moss-rock into a sort of bowl and then push my arm in up to my elbow. As I press in the liquid gets increasingly colder and the sponges get thinner.

Once my arm is well immersed into the material I push and move the moss-rocks easily to the side. I look inside of this cavity I have created but in the near pitch darkness of the hole I can see nothing. I look up to the sky to look for any indication of the sun but the box seems to go up about fifty feet before being thrown into darkness.

I can think of only one way to achieve light and so begin to look around through the mist for some small piece of rock from the walls around me. I continue looking for a few unsuccessful minutes before abandoning the hope and sitting back against the ground, wondering what to do. I sit in that position for a moment before I feel something very hard collide with the top of my head. I grab at my scalp, uttering a cry and rub the stinging spot. I look around to see what may have fallen and see it about a foot away: a large, thin stone about seven inches long.

I look up at the sky, trying to see where it may have fallen from, but can see only the darkness that surrounds the box. I grab the stone and hold it in both hands, covering most of the surface as it begins to heat up. I hold for as long as I can stand before I drop it and thrust my hands into the moss to help cool them down.

The stone sits in front of me, shining so brightly that I can't quite look directly at it without burning its image into my eyes. I check my hands to make sure there are no signs of burns before I rip a handful of the pale moss out of the ground and fashion it into a sort of handle for my stone torch so that I can hold it without burning my hand.

This idea works well and I take my new light over to the hole in the gourd I have created. I move my light over the surface of the void and look down into it, seeing only moss but for a small reflective glow at the very bottom of the chasm.

This means that there may be water at the bottom of all of this. I quickly set down my torch to continue clearing away the spongy rock in the hopes that I may find something at the bottom. I work for a few moments fashioning not only a large hole in the center of the enclosure but also a slope I can ease into to get a better look at the pool and whatever may be below it.

I grab my torch and walk down the slope to the surface of my newly uncovered pond. I look over the somewhat unsettled water to see that it is completely unclouded, making it the first thing in this room that is actually able to be seen through. The pool seems to extend for something like twenty or so feet. The bottom of the pool appears to be covered with the same somewhat mossy, somewhat rocky sort of substance as covering the ground here, but I can also see that one of the four walls only goes down about ten feet before ending abruptly and cleanly.

I don't know if this means there's a way out, but looking around my room I don't see anything else promising, and so I decide to try and dive into the water. I back out away from the pool until I am on the raised slope, grab my torch firmly in my hand, and jump.

My entire body and all of my clothes are instantly drenched as I plunge into the freezing water, falling deeply into it. Then, suddenly, I am out of the water, having only been in for a second. I'm falling for a moment before crashing into the mossy floor. I look up from where I feel and see the water collected against the ceiling, a thin beam of dim light extending through the center of moss up above.

I once again stand up against the moss and again look around. My hopes are confirmed when I see that one of the walls does indeed end and a short passageway extends under it. I hold my torch in front of me and walk slowly down this new path. I see a small door at the end. Directly to the right of the door a note is attached to the wall.

Tentatively, I reach out and pluck the note off its hook, adding light blue marks to the page though no burn is noticeable. The note carries a short message written in black ink.

Peri,
Walk through this door and begin.
Take notes. Take direction. Give direction.
Get to the end.

II

The message confuses me for a number of reasons. Who is Peri? I suddenly realize that I don't know what my own name is, I have no idea who I am. Why do I understand some things, like words for rock or water, but not other things, like who or where I am? In addition to this, what does the note mean by "begin?" Begin what? What is this "end?" Is there some reason I wouldn't get there? Why should I get there? Who wrote this note? Is Peri someone else, and should I have left the note for him? Maybe Peri is a girl, why do I know what a girl is? What is a girl?

I begin to feel a headache coming on and drop the note into the moss below me. Using my free hand I rub my temples while resting my torch hand against the door, relieved to feel that it is wooden and thus leaves no marks. I think for a second and then decide to open the door in front of me.

I stand squarely before it and grab the knob. Interestingly enough, the knob is made of the stone material and begins to glow under my grip. I turn it and then pull back the door quickly. I drop my torch and reach up to try and cover my eyes and ears at the same time as both a blindingly bright light invades the darkness of the dark room and a cacophonous sound blasts all around me.

I stand there bathed in the light flooding into the room through the doorway until my eyes adjust enough to take a cautious look outside. I duck my head through the portal and blink in the harsh light seeming to come from every direction. The door opens into a wide box canyon filled with vegetation. There are a few round hills rolling along the ground, all full of tall, luscious, green grass that comes up to my calf. There is a forest in the distance that towers into the air, covering the horizon in a waving, glistening sea of leaves. The light I had mistaken as coming from everywhere is in fact coming from the sun, which stands high in the sky shining from directly above the doorway I am standing in. It glistens into a large pond to my right to produce a surreal hazy white glow over the entire area. Just past the pond and hills I can see walls.

The walls continue here, and I have a feeling that if I can somehow find a way out of this canyon I'll only escape to another boxed in area. The walls go up for miles in the air as I assume the last ones did. They're made of the same smooth, dark stone material, which means there's no hope of climbing up the walls to get above the enclosed space. Besides, for all I know I would only find more walls above these walls.

I wonder if maybe these walls will glow if I touch them like the others I had passed through. I take a few steps onto the grassy surface out of the doorway and face the wall. The ground seems just as springy as before, and bending down I can see that the grass is rooted in the spongy rock material. I look back up at the wall and press my hand against it for just a moment. I can see a clearly evident handprint against the smooth surface, a blue glow mingling with the whiter haze in the air.

Looking at the glow I suddenly remember that I dropped my torch in the doorway. Based on the lighting here I'm not likely to need it, but I decide to keep it nearby just in case I have more digging to do. I walk back and pick up the light, placing it into a-

A what? There is a hole in the pants I'm wearing. Why do I know about these pants but not what these holes are called? I think about this for a moment before a word arises into my mind as to what the hole is called. A "Pah-kit." I put my torch into my pahkit and turn to head toward the pond.

As I walk in the spongy grass I decide that the ground needs a name too. I think for a few seconds, waiting for the word to be supplied to me, but after a few minutes of intense concentration I still hear nothing. I assume this means that the ground simply does not have a name. *That's okay*, I decide in my mind, *I simply need to come up with my own name for it*. I ponder what sorts of names I could give it, trying to find the right match. It's not quite "dirt," but "mud" also doesn't fit. I don't like "soil," "earth," or "squash," no, all those words seem to be for something else. They all have something about them that doesn't fit this ground. They are all...

living. That feels right, all those words are living, and this material is something else, but what is it?

I try and think hard of what not living is, what is the thing that is opposite of living? I'm very angry at not being able to come up with such a word, and decide to forget about it for now and try to learn more about where I am, whether I have names or not.

As I'm coming up to the pond I look over its surface, which is as still as... glass? Yes, it is still as glass. Unlike the water in the cave I was in before, this water is not clear, but rather cloudy and very dark. Because of this, I can see a reflection of my surroundings off its still veneer of water. Looking over it, I see suddenly there's a face looking at me from under the water. The person there screams and runs away when he sees me, but I barely see him as I quickly scream in panic as soon as I see him, falling back away from the water.

I feel my chest thumping as I breathe heavily, still terrified of whoever it is I just saw. This is the first person I have seen since I woke up in the cave. I slowly move back towards the edge of the pool and look over the surface. I catch my breath as I again see the same man, but this time he looks scared and nervous, which is exactly how I feel. I sit there a moment sizing up the man in the water, noticing that he looks a bit suspicious and unsure of me. I'm not going to hurt him, I just don't want him to hurt me.

I decide I should probably let him know that. I try to speak, but just as I open my mouth the man does as well. I quickly close it but the man does too. I wait there a few moments, holding eye contact, both sides daring the other to speak first until finally I decide I'm wasting my time. "I'm not going to hurt you," I say, and am immediately told the same by the man in the water. "Oh," I say, and so does the man. "I'm sorry," we both say, "I didn't mean to interrupt you."

I move to cover my mouth, but at the same moment the man makes the same movement. It's amazing! This man keeps in perfect tandem with me, no matter what I do. I raise my eyebrow at the man, and he does the same. I sit for a moment, and then reach my hand out towards the water, a bit nervous as I see the man doing the same towards me. My hand meets with the water, sending out ripples across the pond and making contact with the man's hand. I go to grab his hand but then feel nothing. The man in the pond looks confused, which is how I feel. I can see my hand below the surface of the water, but I can't see where the man's hand has gone, his arm seems to simply disappear into my own.

I pull my arm back out of the water, dripping over the image of the man, which makes his appearance greatly distorted. He seems concerned about this, but he has apparently regained his hand as it is now reattached to his shoulder.

I've spent long enough here with this strange man, so I decide to bid him farewell and explore the rest of the canyon. I go to wave at him as he does the same to me, and we both go our separate ways on either side of the pond's surface.

Turning away from the pond, I notice someone moving in the distance at a great speed. The figure runs behind a hill where I can no longer see it. I begin running toward the spot so as to find who else is in this empty world besides myself and the man in the water. I run up the hill and scan the valley, looking for any sign of the person but can see nothing.

I decide to run the direction I had seen him going, perhaps I will catch up to him or find some evidence of where he'd gone. I run and notice that the woods are coming closer and closer, did he go into there? *Perhaps*, I think, but decide to fix my eyes to the ground to look for footprints, hoping the figure had indeed gone this way.
I am nearly to the edge of the forest when I hear a scream to my left. I immediately turn and run down the edge of the tree line trying to find the source of this noise. It doesn't take me long before I see him again, the figure who had been running on the hill. His skin is strange, a dark gray, like the color of the walls, and his clothes are the same color. Despite this, he moves just as fluidly as myself, and he is moving a lot.

I can now see why he was screaming so loudly that he could be heard across the valley. He is sinking. The mossy rock that I still hadn't come up with a name for is rising up like tendrils, latching onto him all over his body and pulling him downwards. It opens up and pulls the man into its maw. The man is fighting and screaming, flailing his arms around, but it doesn't seem to be doing any good. He is slowly descending into the spongy material.

After about a minute the man has been fully engulfed and the ground closes its cavity, grass suddenly reappearing over the now smooth surface. I stand there, a bit stunned, unsure of what happened. The man certainly didn't seem to like what had happened, but I wasn't sure why that was. What is so bad about the ground? Why is it so bad to be buried?

I'm not sure, after all I'm brand new to this world and its mysteries, but maybe this man had been there for weeks, or maybe even years. He surely knew more about the world than I do, for I know nothing. *I don't know how to respond to the ground eating the man, but he was scared. No,* I think, *scared isn't the right word, it's not enough. No, the right word is…* I think for a few seconds, and then the word comes to me, *terrified. That man was terrified of the ground.* Maybe terrified is what everyone thinks of the ground. The man who was eaten, the man in the water, and maybe me.

Am I terrified? No, but I suppose I should be, since he was. *Yes,* I decide, *I should be terrified of the ground.* And suddenly my mind seems clearer, for now I know how to respond to the ground, and in that moment, its name also came to me. I know what the opposite of living is now. The ground, the spongy, mossy, rocky ground is named *Death*.

III

I smile to myself, now knowing both what "Death" is and how to respond to it. I look around the valley and all the death within it, it seems to make up the ground for everything, a base for everything else to grow up out of and be terrified of.

As I am looking out over the loamy death, I feel a sudden pain in my stomach and it makes a low roaring noise. I don't know how I know what this means, but I immediately begin looking around for food. I head back to the pond, greet the man in the water as he waves back at me, and then jump into the water myself. I swim for a moment, looking around to see if there is anything edible here. I see small creatures swimming around with me, *Fish*, they're called. I suppose I could catch the fish and eat them, but I don't think they would be very good, so I drift back up to the surface of the water and leave the pond.

I decide the next best option for food is likely the forest, so I begin walking that direction. On the edge of the trees is a particularly large oak. The tree extends high into the air and is so wide that even were I two people I wouldn't be able to extend my arms completely around its trunk. The tree *is* large, but that's not what gets my attention, for many of the trees here are equally big and some even bigger. What really gets my attention is the note attached to the front of the tree.

The note is a single page nailed into the wood in the same way as the note I found in the cave telling me to go out the door. I pluck the note from its fitting and read what is inscribed. It says:

Peri,
Food can be found inside the forest.
Do not eat spotted berries or mushrooms.
Take notes. Take direction. Give direction.

Again the note begins with Peri. I wonder if this is a word that means something I haven't yet come across. Maybe it will become clear eventually. I read the rest of the note and peer into the dark woods. I pull my torch out of my pahkit and walk cautiously forward, looking all around for any berries or nuts throughout that might be food. I happen across a bush full of berries and after quickly making sure they have no spots, I begin picking and eating them as quickly as I can manage.

Once I have eaten enough to be satisfied, I turn to head back out of the forest, but as I look around, I suddenly cannot remember which way I came in from. I try to look through the large, thick trees to find some ray of light from the way out, but none is forthcoming and soon I am confronted with the realization that I am lost.

I can feel my chest thumping hard again as it had before as I am suddenly very frightened by the thought of what may happen if I cannot leave this forest. Will I be able to reach the "end" that the first note spoke of? Will the death overtake me and maybe even consume me as it had the man I had seen? How long will I be stuck?

I decide it isn't doing me any good to just sit there, and if the death is going to come for me that means I should try and move, maybe even run away as the man had. I choose a direction and begin walking, caring not where it will take me so long as it will take me somewhere that ends up out of these woods. I walk for many minutes, crunching over the layer of leaves built up over the death on the forest floor. The woods continue to grow darker as I keep walking on, making the blue glow of my torch seem brighter and brighter.

I continue to walk until finally, mercifully, after what feels like hours of pointless wandering, I come to a clearing. It is made up like a semicircle without any trees. There are flowers and grass growing here, and small bugs flying happily and lazily in the sunlight that just barely lights the area from over the roof of tree cover. On the other side of the clearing, there is the wall. I walk into the clearing and sit down for a moment. Normally I wouldn't be very happy to have come across another wall, but finding one in the forest means I can walk along it until I come out of the forest as soon as I'm ready.

Peri

I rest for a few moments and then stand and begin following the wall back into the forest. I keep the wall close, never more than one tree away so that I can easily see it when I need to. As it begins to get darker I notice the dark gray of the stone wall getting increasingly harder to see. I don't want to get lost again, so I walk over to the wall and placed my hand against it long enough to get a strong, bright blue glow against its surface that I can easily see from many feet away.

I continue in this way, walking along the wall, leaving a handprint against it every five feet or so. I walk for what feels like around an hour when I come across a clearing that looks exactly like the one I had stumbled upon before. This seems strange, but still seeing no real way out of the forest I continue to walk in the direction I had been going. The path starts getting dark again and I move to place a handprint on the wall, when I see that one is already there, identical to my own. Looking down the wall I can see that every five or six feet is another handprint, exactly how I had laid them out.

Impossibly, I have somehow managed to move in a circle before I came out of the forest. I run through the woods until I come to the clearing again, and this time I look and can see where I had sat the first time I had arrived there. I can see my footprints leading back into the forest from where I now stand. I am moving in a loop, but I've been going the same direction the entire time! I continue to run through the woods, the same way, the opposite direction, even entirely new ways that I had never seen before, but I keep ending up back at the clearing against the wall.

I run for hours until I collapse against the grass and flowers as I again come across the clearing. I've lost track of the number of times I've stumbled into this place that has become horrible to me. I can't seem to get out of it, no matter where I go I always come back. As I lie there, my stomach once again roars and I realize I am hungry again.

I look around for any food in this clearing I have come to despise. I notice a strange plant growing on the ground. I look down at it. It seems to be growing in a patch with ten or twelve individual heads. The plant is short and close to the ground, growing upwards as a stalk before expanding in a bulbous head. The entire plant is a light tan and looks like it might be edible.

I think back to the last note I read, it said not to eat speckled berries or mushrooms. This plant certainly isn't a berry, and I have no idea what a mushroom is, so I decide that the tan plants should be safe and begin picking them. I don't know what the name of my plant is, so I decide to simply call it a fungus as that's the word that pops into my head. I take the funguses and break them into smaller pieces in the grass. I pick some of the flowers around me and add some of the petals in with my little meal. I call my creation "salad" and begin to eat.

The salad soon fills my empty stomach and I lie back in the grass, feeling drowsy after so much walking and a meal. I fall asleep to the gentle light of the sun drifting over the trees, which wave melodically to the wind.

I wake up some time later to my stomach feeling as though it is squeezing and expanding. I rolled over in the grass and grab my abdomen, curling into a ball as a low moan escapes from my mouth. The pain coming from my stomach is excruciating, feeling as though it may implode, taking me with it.

Suddenly I realize what it must be. I look over at the patch of funguses in the grass a few feet away. Though I took quite a few of the plants there were still a few heads peaking up among the flowers. I grab the nearest one as my stomach rolls back in a contraction. Clutching the soft material, I begin to tear apart the head. I see with horror that in the center of the fungus is a pale gray substance making up the middle of the stalk and the head.

I easily recognize the substance.

It is death.

No sooner do I have this realization than I feel a sudden force from my neck pulling my head back towards the grass. Soon my arms and legs are pinned to the ground, and what feels like ropes are taut over my stomach, clutching tighter. I move my head as far as I can with the restraint to look over at my wrist. What I see fills me with dread, it terrifies me.

The death rises out of the ground to form a sort of cord binding my hands to the ground, where it would probably soon begin pulling me into itself. *I am going to die*, I think as the death winds tighter and tighter. It makes the war raging in my stomach feel even worse and my body naturally begins curling up again against the death holding me firmly to the ground, exposed and defenseless.

My stomach continues to spin, and more death continues to clutch at me. Soon a wide strip of the grey moss comes up and covers my eyes, succinctly cutting out all light and vision. I scream out, struggling against the death furiously but unable to get away. I'm getting tired, my limbs growing weak. The pain emanating from my stomach continues to churn and grow, now feeling like it is burning through my throat.

The blend of the death restricting my chest and my inability to properly use my throat causes me to start coughing, and then I can't stop. I gasp for breath as the death overwhelms my body. Suddenly in the middle of coughing I feel a glob of a gooey substance, likely death, jump into my mouth. My body can't take it anymore and my chest begins to surge and whatever is in my stomach is suddenly rushing into my throat and out of my mouth.

The taste is disgusting, acidic and rancid, like something rotten. The only thing worse than this taste is the smell entering my barely open nostrils. I feel as though I am being attacked by the senses overloading my system and begin to feel myself passing out. I struggle to retain consciousness, when the bonds on my chest and limbs begin to alleviate.

I struggle again, fighting against the death clutching me to the ground. I wrestle with the sentient shackles for a few moments until I am finally free, lying in the grass panting. The world is spinning in circles and I notice annoying dots of light clouding my vision as I lie there. I don't move until the world stops swirling and I can see properly.

Even after waiting for so long, when I do decide to sit up the lights return and I have to take another few seconds before I can fully stand. I do finally manage to get up and process just what has happened. I turn back to the funguses still growing in the grass.

I have no doubt any longer that these plants are the mushrooms I read about in the note at the entrance to the forest and I stomp on each one as firmly as I can, grinding them into the death below. I then bend down, pull a large amount of grass up and bury the mushrooms under it. I want to do more to show my resentment to the plant that tried so hard to hurt me and make the death take me, but I can think of nothing else, so I simply turn away from the mound I have created.

IV

My wrath satisfied, I must now decide what to do to go on. I can likely find some more berries in the woods, but unless I find a way out of the endless cycle the clearing creates, I will be stuck here. Eventually I will eat all the berries, and in one way or another, the death will begin to rise again and take me over, and I may not be as lucky the second time. I consider climbing one of the trees to see if I can find the way out from higher up, but even the lowest limbs are far above my head, and looking up at how high the trees went, I would need to climb for what looked like miles before I got above the trees enough to see beyond them.

The idea of being that high scares me for some reason, it is a similar feeling to the terrified one the death caused. No, climbing the trees isn't a good idea. I look into the woods, trying to see if there is a way out, but, as I expected, all I see are dark shadows and trees.

Turning back to the wall, I see again the mound of grass and mushroom I created. I think back on the note warning me of the vile plant. It knew that the mushrooms were bad, even though I didn't know what mushrooms even were. Maybe it knows how I am meant to get out of here too, maybe it said something that didn't make sense before, but that I could figure out now. I pull up a mental image of the note and what it said.

Peri,
Food can be found inside the forest.
Do not eat spotted berries or mushrooms.
Take notes. Take direction. Give direction.

I still haven't seen any spotted berries, but I really don't think that has anything to do with getting out of here. I wonder what the sentences at the bottom of the page mean. It had been on the first note as well, is it a message? "Take notes." What does that mean? Am I supposed to have kept both the pages I found? I hope it means something else, I left both where I found them, and if I can't get out of this forest I'll never be able to retrieve them.

"Take direction. Give direction." This is equally confusing. I had taken the direction the notes gave me, but who was I supposed to give direction to? I had only come across two people in this world, and one is stuck in the pond where I can't get while the other had been eaten by death. I wonder if I'm supposed to make paper notes like the ones I had gotten and pin them around for other people to find. I wouldn't have a problem doing this, but I don't have any paper and don't know where I can get any.

I try to solve the problem but only end up giving myself a headache when it comes to me. I don't know for sure that it will actually help anybody, but I do know one way I can leave notes. I run over to the wall at the edge of the clearing and begin tracing out a message. Using my finger, I write a short letter on the wall. I say that there is food to be found in the forest, and I make a small picture of a mushroom so that anybody reading the note will know what they are and stay away from them. I hope they won't eat them as I had, I now know just how brutal the death can be if given the chance. I also include a bit of information about the man in the water, saying that he is nice and will leave you alone, I think he's just lonely. On the end I write a quick sentence warning of the death and what it can do.

I've nearly finished my note when I again remember the last sentences on my own notes. I don't know for sure if they're important, but I decide I shouldn't risk it and write the three quick messages at the bottom of the page. I take a step back, not really sure what I'm expecting but hoping a way out of this forest will somehow be revealed.

Nothing happens.

After a few minutes of nothing pass, I begin to grow annoyed and walk back up to my note. I go over all the information I put into it and can't figure out what is missing. I have given the direction, I have written a note, it has even more information than I'd been given, what's missing?

I begin to turn away, sure that I've wasted my time tracing blue all over the wall, when it occurs to me I have indeed forgotten one element of the note. Both of my notes had started with the word "Peri." I still don't know for sure what that word means, but it had been on both, so it's probably important in some way. I wonder if I'm supposed to write it at the top of my page as well, but don't, it feels wrong. I may not know for certain just what "Peri" means, but I do feel like it's meant to just maybe be me.

I look at the note on the wall, shining out towards my face, and extend my finger, not to the top, but to the bottom of the letter. There, I simply trace out "From Peri." and lower my hand.

Immediately there is a noise roaring in my ears and the wind picks up, even in the tree-covered clearing. I stand there, grass and flowers being whipped around in the wind. My mound of mushrooms and grass is grabbed by the gusting force and disappears into the trees. I kneel down and clutch the grass at my feet frantically, hoping not to be carried away when I hear a ripping noise above me. I look up towards the sound, and can see my note on the wall coming off the dark rock. The words extend away from the wall and seemed to change. They stop glowing blue and instead change to a dull black, and it almost appears as though the air surrounding the words is consolidating into a skin.

No, I think, *not skin. It's paper.*

The note I wrote onto the wall is peeling off into an actual page of paper with inky black words. I can even see the small illustration of a mushroom moving over onto the paper. The page peels completely off the wall, its entire message contained, and then it flies directly upwards. I stare up at the sky, watching it disappear over the trees until I can no longer see it in the sunlight.

I look back downwards, letting go of the grass I had so adamantly clung to, and gasp audibly. The wall in front of me has opened up, creating a doorway that extends ten feet into the air. There's no door, but rather a dark staircase descending around a corner into blackness. I take a deep breath, stand up, and begin to walk downstairs.

The first few steps into the tunnel are easy, light still pools in from behind, an exit, albeit it a poor one, is close by, and I can clearly see the path. However, as soon as I turn the corner all of these things are lost. I turn around but can see no light coming in from the corner. I then know that I am again trapped in the same way I had been in the forest.

So, I walk. I walk and walk without any vision other than that of my torch, feeling more than seeing that I am moving downwards in a spiral with every step. Eventually the tunnel stops moving in a circle and I walk forward for a bit. Shortly after the tunnel straightens out and I see a speck of light in the distance. As I pick up my pace the spot begins growing larger and larger.

I am about halfway down the long, straight tunnel when I hear a crackling noise to my right. I casually glance over towards the wall, holding my torch out in front of me. After a moment of watching the wall I notice what looks like the slightest of movements. I'm confused, but sure that I have seen something I take a few steps over to the wall, examining it closer up with my torch.

Again I see nothing on the wall, so I turn back to the path, deciding that whatever noises I heard or movements I had seen were probably just my imagination. Just as I turn away though, I hear another noise and whirl my head around, seeing what could only be an arm reaching directly out of the wall at me. I give a startled yell and fall away from the wall a few feet, tripping onto the ground.

I look at the hand, stretched out toward me. It's made of the same dark gray stone as the wall it's coming out of, but it's moving plenty more than most stones I have seen. The hand continues to stretch out toward me, reaching out as far as its length will allow. It continues in that position for an instant and then retracts back into the wall, leaving no sign it had existed at all.

I stumble to my feet and begin running towards the doorway, hoping its light will somehow protect me. As I run I can hear more creaking from the walls on either side. Turning to each side I see that now whole beings have emerged from the walls and are now running after me. There have to be dozens of the stone people, all the same dull, dark gray color, and all running for me.

I am forty feet from the doorway when hands begin rising up from the floor between me and the light. They grab at me as I run past them, one of them manages to get a good hold on my shoe and

I feel it come cleanly off my foot as I continue to run, causing blue footprints to appear on the hard stone flooring beneath me. I am only about ten feet away and the flailing arms are now covering the ground directly in front of the doorway while now hundreds of people are sprinting towards me from behind. I add an extra burst of speed, not sure what these people can possibly want, and then jump.

I only barely clear the hands as they lung and snatch at my legs, and then I am outside. No sooner do I pass through the doorway than it closes up as though some great force has pulled it closed. I stand there, facing the now blank wall, when from its other side I can hear a thunderous pounding, like hammers banging into the wall. I second later I realize this must be all the people colliding with the wall at the end of their sprint, and for a moment I'm concerned they will pass directly through and continue pursuing me on this side of the wall. I wait cautiously for a few seconds, and then let go a deep breath when nothing emerges from the wall.

V

I turn around and for the first time take a look at where I have come. It looks similar to the valley I was in a while ago, with grass and flowers growing up out of the death and pools of water spread around. However, unlike the valley, this area is not a box canyon, nor is it a valley. Rather this area is shaped like a jagged line with one long path passing up and down, left and right as the land moves. The walls still rise up on either side, but here they only seem to extend upwards a few dozen feet. Still far too high to scale or see over, but not so high that they disappear among the clouds as before.

Looking to my left I see a sort of recess in the stone wall and I walk over to it. There is a bowl of water cut into the alcove itself, and looking down into it I see my friend, the man in the water. Somehow he has managed to leave the pond in the valley and come into this very small source of water in the wall here.

I wave enthusiastically at the man, smiling as I see him do the same. We both fumble over our words as we try to greet one another but, as before, somehow always say the same thing at the same moment. I look over at the long path I will need to cross to move on, and glancing back at the man in the water I can see he is doing the same. I give him a wry smile, which he returns, and then I remember I am meant to take notes.

I turn to the wall I came through, and though I don't want to touch anything that could spring out arms suddenly, I begin detailing to whomever will read this that people can come out of the wall and he should be wary that they will try to grab him. I also write that the man in the water has managed to come here with me, and I draw an arrow over to the alcove where his bowl is. As I do, I can see him doing the same, only towards me, and for a moment I am happy. The man in the water wants people to know that I am here, and I think that is very sweet.

Peri

I smile once more at the man, and realize as he smiles back at me that this man really is my friend. I do like him indeed. Then, I wave farewell and begin walking down the hill and slightly to the right as the path veers off. I walk for a few minutes while keeping my eyes peeled for any sign of a note, some food (my stomach has begun rumbling lowly again), and any movement from the walls, but I see no sign of any of these.

Once I reach the bottom of the hill I come across another pond, this one full of large orange fish swimming quietly around near the surface. I take a moment to look at these fish as they swim around before coming closer and walking into the water. I can see the man in the water looking up at me from his place among the fish. One orange fish comes up to me and nips at my legs, which tickles, causing me to jerk my legs out of the water, which in turn scares the fish and they scatter in all directions, fast as lightning.

I laugh a little, watching them scuttle away so quickly, and look at a small island sitting in the center of the pond. I walk through the water towards it, the liquid rising to my waist as I go further into it. I reach the island and sit down in a nook that seems perfectly created for just this purpose. There is some soft moss, real moss, not death, to sit on, a large rock I can rest against, a tree hanging just over the rock that provided shade, and the water where I can place my feet and let the fish nibble my toes.

I sit there, looking out at the path forward, resting in the soft sunlight and cool water, allowing myself to relax without fear of people coming, screaming out of the walls to get me or worried the death would rise up and take me over. I look over and see a small patch of fruits growing on a vine around the tree, and pick a few of the ripe plants to nibble them as I sit against the rock.

I continue to eat while slowly drifting off to sleep in the warm air. I sleep for what I imagine must be a few hours, but when I wake the sun hasn't moved at all. This is strange I am fairly certain. I feel as though it should have moved somehow. Now that I'm thinking about it, I can't remember the sun moving at all. Why do I feel like it should have been?

I can't say for certain, all I know is that it *should* have moved, and it hasn't. I decide not to bother about it for now and instead take some time to think about where I am and what I should do. I could continue walking down the path, and probably find another place to go after that. I could also just stay here, enjoy the shade and warmth, the fruits and the water I could have any time I want. I look around, there are quite a few ponds here, I could see the man in the water whenever I wanted, and maybe he and I could even find a way to get him out of the water so we could play together.

Yes, I could do that. That sounds very nice I decide. I think I'll do just that. For now, I eat another fruit.

I spent a very long time in that place, getting to know all its nooks and crannies. I would spend hours looking through the forests, swimming in the ponds, running up the hills and rolling back down them. I became friends with the fish in all the bodies of water, giving each of them names and knowing each one by sight. I also found many small animals in the woods scattered around. There were small, furry creatures of all sort of shapes and sizes. They all ate nuts and berries, so I always shared my food with them. They would come out and play whenever they saw me.

I'd also spend my time there eating and finding new foods. I was always very careful to break apart new foods before I ate it, to check if there was any death within them as there had been with the mushrooms. Occasionally I would find such a plant and I would immediately destroy all of it I could find, sometimes searching the forests and hills for hours looking for any signs of them. In this way, I saved myself and my animal friends from suffering from the toxic effects of the death.

And yet, for all my attempts to protect them, occasionally I would notice my friends had disappeared, or sometimes even see the death rise up from the ground and absorb them. It always made me very sad, and angry, to lose my friends, but I didn't know what I could do against the death. It was everywhere around me, it wasn't as though I could actually get away from it, and when it struck, I was powerless against it. The animals didn't seem to have any defense against it either. They would run away whenever the long, pale grey tendrils rose out of the earth, but it always caught them, I never saw one get away as I had.

I decided while I was here that I do not like the death. Before I had been terrified of it, but that was simply because the man who had died had been terrified and I felt that was appropriate. Now I know it a little better, and I don't like it. I am going to escape this death in whatever ways I can, I won't let it get me. Any time I saw any death beginning to bubble up around me or my friends, I would throw grass, splash water, or throw rocks at it, trying to suppress it. Occasionally I was successful, and the death crept back into the ground, but more often my efforts proved in vain, and one of my friends would disappear under the surface.

So I spent time examining the death. It was a little bit frightening, but I decided that to truly escape death I would need to understand just what it was. I would pull handfuls of death up from the ground and test it against different materials.

Grass would simply take root in death and grow taller, energized by the countless souls that passed into death. Rocks seemed to have no effect on the death, they both simply sat on each other without reacting. If placed in water the death became extremely slippery and elongated into a noodle form and floated to the surface. Sunlight made the death hot, but otherwise didn't seem to affect it much. My skin would crinkle and get spots if I left patches of death on it for too long, though interestingly enough my palm remained unaffected, even though I covered the handle of my torch with death.

But then, the torch was made of the dark rock of the walls, and the two materials had strange effects on each other. I noticed in dark areas covered by trees where there was no grass that the death would sometimes glow slightly where it met the wall. It wasn't the same as the blue glow my hands caused against the dark stone walls, this light was orange, and it was very dim. It would be invisible entirely if the death and wall weren't so dull in comparison. I also saw once that the death seemed to be eating away at the base of the wall. I didn't know why these two materials reacted so strangely with one another, but I did know that they could be very dangerous, so I decided to try and stay away from the walls at the spots where there were no grass covering the death.

Of course, I was watching the walls for an entirely different reason anyway. I was still very careful to keep an eye out for any movement the walls may be producing, and occasionally my caution proved valuable. Once or twice I would see a rogue arm flailing out of the walls grabbing at whatever may be close, even if there was nothing at all, before settling down after a few minutes. Sometimes though, I would see a face, or what looked like an entire body, trying to press out of the stone wall. They would struggle in the rock as though held back by some sort of curtain, pressing forward towards me violently. The faces would scream silently into the stone surface, leaving me many visions which provided ample fuel for nightmares when I slept.

Even with this unfortunate risk though, I only rarely saw the people in the walls, and I actually spent quite a bit on time at the walls. At first I had been afraid to go anywhere near them, but as time passed and I decided that the threats emanating from them were minimal, I began to draw on them. I would wake up, eat a small meal of berries and nuts, and then go to the walls and etch out the sights I saw around me. I would draw my friends, the animals, or the stream, trees, clouds in the sky above, or the man in the water, who was my best friend. I filled the walls with glowing blue symbols on all the sides of the area. I spent more time drawing on the walls than doing anything else.

Since the time I decided to stay here I managed to cover all the grounds of the walls. From the spot where I had come into this forested and watered patch between the walls, all the way to the opposite side, beyond the woods. On all sides my drawings were to be seen, but no door or other exit was evident. This didn't really surprise me, as it seemed every exit way was carefully hidden or disguised in my past wanderings. It also didn't concern me much. If no way out wanted to be found, I wouldn't look for it. I was going to escape death, but I didn't have to escape this little domain, my little domain.

I was the master here, the ruler and lord. I decided when I slept or ate, I chose when and where to explore, or what to play, or even what to draw. I took notes occasionally, but not because I was told to but more because I wanted to remember something important. I would draw pictures of death filled plants I found, mark spots where I had seen arms or faces coming through the walls, or write up which foods tasted best together. The death may be bigger than me, but I was learning how to defeat it, and in the end *I* would be the last one standing.

Occasionally I would sit down in my island seat and have a long conversation with the man in the water. Of course this was always difficult because we still managed to always speak over one another, but even still I could see what he was thinking through the looks in his eyes or the way his mouth turned upwards when I told a joke. He would of course tell me jokes as well, and I would always laugh with him, especially since I would say the same thing at the same moment.

The man in the water was very nice to me, and he seemed to always be ready for me. I would purposely pretend to go to sleep when he would, and then try to surprise him, but he always woke up just in time to catch me. He and I would watch the fish as they bustled about under the water, or conduct experiments on death together, or whatever we could find to do. He enjoyed drawing as much as I did, and we would both borrow from the same subjects all around in the woods or ponds.

I was quite glad that he wanted to stay in this spot, without moving ahead, like me, with me. I loved the animals and fish, but the man in the water was far easier to speak with, and I could see what he felt on different subjects much easier with his human face than the furry ones of the small animals.

It was always have a comfort to have a friend around so often, but sometimes he would have to leave. I discovered while living here that sometimes the sky clouds collected so much that they cover the sky in a dark roof that looks a lot like the walls around me. And sometimes, when the clouds get dark like this, water would fall out of them.

The first time this happened I was very excited, I danced around in the water and ran over to the pond to see what the man in the water thought about it. I was sure he would be very excited to see so much water, he lived in water after all! But when I got to the pond he was nowhere to be found. I looked everywhere but I just couldn't find him. I wondered if maybe the water scared him somehow, though I didn't know why it would, and then the water scared me too.

While I was sitting over the pond, looking for the man in the water, suddenly there was a bright flash of light that illuminated all the area, so bright it made my glowing drawings look dim. The light isn't what scared me most though, but rather shortly after this light, a deep, roaring, explosion of a noise burst forth from the sky, making me grab my ears and fall to the ground.

Suddenly the water terrified me as much as the death and I ran into the woods to get out of it. I sat there for a while, surrounded by a few of my friends while we all waited for the water to stop coming down. We were all soaking wet and cold by the time it finally did, and the clouds cleared away to show the sun brightly shining again.

The sun quickly dried everything up and made it feel warm again, but I suppose somehow some death must have slipped into my nose, for it was very stuffy and I kept sneezing for quite a while after the storm. I ran back to the pond and saw that the man in the water was back, which made me feel a lot better. I also laughed when I saw that the man was sneezing and stuffy too, just like me. The fish would scatter whenever we both gave an explosive sneeze and then laughed at each other, and then laughed even more at the fish's panic at nothing.

Those were very good times, living in that little area, my area, for such a long time. In that glade we had death, but it didn't touch me, and my friends were mostly spared from it too. My drawings glowed out whenever the clouds darkened the glade, and the man in the water and I played for hours. I enjoyed my time then, and wish it could have continued forever, but unfortunately, it couldn't. Few things ever do.

VI

Time went on with little care or concern and I kept to my somewhat schedule. I would draw on the walls, eat, sleep, do experiments, or whatever else I wanted, whenever I felt like it. Nothing ever changed or kept me from doing such things, until once when I was exploring the woods as I had thousands of times before.

I had been in the woods for hours, sometimes running or walking through the trails I knew so well, sometimes sitting and watching the sunlight drift through the canopy of leaves. I had been accompanied by many animals all the while I was in the forest, and had been talking with them throughout. But when I turn to them at one point, I suddenly notice they aren't there.

I turn all around, looking up and around all of the trees, but I can't find any of the friends who had been following me around for the past few hours. Where have they gone? And how long have they been missing? They were following me, I know they were, weren't they? I leave the forest, looking for them, and when I leave the boundary of trees, my mouth drops.

I'm facing the wall from which I had entered this glade, the one where the rock had closed up after I had come through, only now, the wall isn't closed. The face of the stone is rippling out from the space I had run through, and as it does a hole in the center of the wall grows larger and large, opening into a pitch black circular portal. I stand there watching the wall open up wider and wider like a mouth for a few seconds, before I notice the sky is darkening again.

Looking up I can see clouds filling up the sky, faster than I've ever seen before. This means that it will begin raining soon, and then the noises and lights will come from the sky. Normally I wouldn't be too frightened by this, I can just hide in the woods until it finishes, but this time the wall is open, and something or somethings could come out of it. In addition, all of my friends have disappeared, so there will be nobody to sit with me to wait out the storm.

I feel my heart begin to beat faster, my breath comes quicker. I don't know what to do in this storm and it's beginning to make me panic. I quickly decide to simply hide in the woods and hope nothing comes out of the hole in the wall that will hurt me. I turn around to go back into the trees when I see that there are no trees in sight.

Much like the animals disappearing a few minutes ago, now the forests have also disappeared. There had been three large forests in this glade, and now there are none, including the one I had been standing just in front of seconds before. I turn back to the wall, has it moved closer? No, that's impossible, it's probably just some optical illusion caused by the hole getting larger. And yet, as I watch, I can see the ground under me seem to be pulled towards the wall, bringing me closer and closer to the hole that seemed about to swallow me up.

I immediately run in the opposite direction I'm being pulled, directly toward the nearest pond I can see, where the man in the water will be. That is, unless he has disappeared as well. Coming to the surface of the pool, I can see that he is still in his home, though he looks very worried. Of course he does, it's about to rain, and he hates the water from the sky and now the wall is opening. He has plenty of reason to be scared, and I do too. Even as I look at the man, the pond begins to lower, draining into who knows where.

I look back at the wall that has now nearly completely opened up. It is getting really close now. I hear a roar from behind me and see to my horror that now the back wall is moving forward at an alarming rate. Soon I would be pressed into the hole opening up. The wall continues to glide against the ground toward me around each jagged corner in the twisting land.

My drawings on the walls begin to fall behind the mobile barrier, each lost to the stone in turn. The hole opening up is now beginning to make its own noise as what sounds like thousands of pounding footsteps emanate from it. The roar of the running people from the cave mix with the roar of grinding rock from the moving wall and each are soon joined by the roar of the sky as the lights flash and water falls. I thought I would soon go deaf with all of the noise surrounding me, and then, just I am sure my ears will explode, the death begins to rise up in long tendrils, thrusting out and grabbing mounds of grass, ripping them up and absorbing them into the grey mass of the floor. Death continues reaching out among the falling water and cacophonous noise and all in all I am sure the end of my short life has come.

The moving wall has now caught up to me, and it begins moving me forward toward the wall that is now a huge entryway. I gets within about five feet of the black abyss when I suddenly stop and the ground stops pulling into the hole. I stand there, facing the blackness so thick no light can penetrate it, while water rains down on my head. I stand there, hearing the pounding footsteps grow louder and louder, expecting an army to come out any moment.

And soon enough, out steps a girl.

That's it, one girl. One, single girl comes out into the rain looking very confused and scared. She looks up at the sky that is letting all its water loose upon her head, and then over at me. We stand there, watching one another a moment, neither person wanting to move too quickly, and then she takes a few steps forward, waving.

I waved back at her, holding my position. The water continues to pour down, and unless I am mistaken it has started falling even harder. The girl gestures for me to come closer, then turns around to stand under the archway of the opening, getting out of the water.

I decide there is nothing she can do to me, and I follow her into the dark but dry tunnel. There we stand, watching one another, maintaining eye contact but not saying anything. The water pours down, the thunder roars, but we are silent.

Finally, when I can take it no longer, I say quietly, "Hi, I'm Peri..." then look down at the ground.

She eyes me for a moment then stutters out, "I...I'm Disha."

I look back at the girl then, and slowly reach out my hand. She eyes it a moment, then takes it and we shake. "It's nice to meet you Disha," I say, then I look around. "Any idea where we're supposed to go now?"

"Don't you have a home?" she asks.

"Well," I sigh, "I did, once." And looking out at the wall that has eaten up the glade that had been my childhood, I feel a stinging mist begin to collect in my eyes. I know the man in the water will be okay, he always is. But I will never again see the animals that had become my friends. The trails and hiding places in the woods and ponds are no more, no, longer can I stay in them. And my drawings, all my drawings are lost, eaten by the dark stone that kept me ever enclosed and always close to the death, so that life could never approach for long. "My home is gone now," I tell Disha. "The walls took it."

Disha seems to understand and she doesn't ask any more questions. We sit in the opening of the cave until the rain stops, and then we try to decide where to go. "What's down this tunnel?" I ask, expecting it to have changed since I came from it.

"A registana," Disha says.

"What is a registana?" I ask, fumbling with the new word.

The girl looks at me, confused by how I could not know such a word. "A registana. You know, registana, with sand everywhere, it is always hot." She tries using her hands to get her idea across, though how this would help I wasn't sure. She continued to explain the concept of a registana, but it was unlike anything I had ever heard of. "It is yellow and orange and red there, and very dusty. And this" here she pointed at the pools of water now at our feet, "never falls from the sky. There is very little of it there."

"A registana doesn't sound very nice," I say.

"It is not always. What kind of place was this?" Disha asks, "Before it was destroyed."

"It was green and golden, with lots of trees and flowers and little animals. There were ponds filled with fish, and they would swim around all day. They were very silly if they were scared. The water also had-" and here I stop. I don't know why, but I don't want to tell Disha about the man in the water. I hadn't looked yet, but he is probably waiting in the puddles all around the ground.

"Had what?" Disha asks.

"Had a little island I would sit at and rest... It was very nice, I would spend hours there sometimes," I say. I don't know why I feel bad about not telling her the truth, but for some reason I feel black and gummy inside, much like the way the death feels when it is wet. I try to ignore the feeling, but it seems ever on the forefront of my mind. I instinctually know I should have told her the truth, and yet, I can't bring myself to do it. The man in the water will remain my secret for now.

"It sounds very nice indeed," Disha says. "So where should we go now? The registana is a wasteland, there is no point in going back there."

"I agree, it doesn't sound like a very good place, but I don't know where else to go," I say, "Our options are a bit limited here, and I haven't gotten any notes in all the time I've been here."

"Notes?"

"Yeah, notes. They're pages that tell you what to do, I make them myself too, though I don't know where they go. They're usually nailed to a tree or something."

"Oh, I have seen those!" Disha says excitedly, "Yes, they are how I found my way out of the registana."

"Yeah," I say, "but like I said I haven't found any." I stand up and look at the very small area outside of the cave. There are only about forty square feet open, and this is completely covered with death and a shallow layer of water. Looking at the walls I see none of my drawings, I had never noticed I hadn't drawn any this close. I do however, see the alcove that was here when I first arrived, where I had seen the man in the water had made it here with me.

I look inside the bowl, surprised to see no water, but rather a black hole. "Hey!" I call out, "Come check this out!"

Disha gets up and runs over to the nook, looking down at the hole. "What is it?"

"I think it may be our way out."

"But we don't know where it goes, it could be anywhere," Disha protests.

"Well, yeah, but we don't have much to lose," I say, gesturing at all glorious forty square feet of dark, grey, damp death and a giant, black hole leading to a wasteland.

"But we would have to jump down a hole," Disha says, "who knows how far we'd fall down? We could die."

"Die?" I ask. "What does that mean?"

Disha's face falls at the question. She points to the ground, "You know this soft stuff?"

"You mean the death?"

"Death, that is what you call it? Has the death ever taken someone over that you've seen?" She asks.

I remember the grey man again, the way the ground climbed over him and swallowed him whole. The terrified way he screamed and the way his face looked as the death closed in over it. I also think about all of my friends that I found in the woods being absorbed, or the friends who just disappeared sometimes, which I knew meant they had been taken while I hadn't been there. "Yeah," I say quietly, "I've seen that."

"Well," Disha says, still looking at the ground, "When that happens, it means they died. It happened a lot in the registana. This death would rise up on really hot days or whenever bugs would bite you."

We both sit there, thinking about the ones we've lost, and wondering silently if going down the hole will kill us. "It doesn't matter," I say after a few moments. "It doesn't matter if it is too far, there's no where else to go, it's too perfect of a way out not to take. I mean, the tunnel obviously isn't the way to go, it just ends up in the registana, and there's no where else to go." Disha looks up at me. "Come on," I continue, "let's take a risk, see what's down there."

The girl seems to ponder this for a while, trying to decide if it is indeed worth the risk, then she looks back down the hole. "Well, then," she says, still looking down into the blackness, "I suppose there isn't anywhere else to go." Then she hops onto the edge of the alcove, and before I can say anything, she jumps into the hole feet first. I barely have time to register this action before she's gone. I laugh a little, then hop in after her.

PART TWO
SUMMER

VII

I fall for a little while, air rushing up all around me and having the faintest feeling of flying. Then out of no where the sun appears directly above me, as though it has fallen through the hole as well and is now falling after me. I look below and with the light of the sun I can now see a blue color. The blue rushes up closer and closer to me and suddenly I fall into it. It takes me a moment as I am surrounded by this blue to realize that it is water. I have fallen into some sort of giant pond.

I swim to the surface and look around for Disha and somewhere to go. I see the answer to both when I turn and see a large island a little ways away. I swim to the shore of the island and walk up on the land. The ground is made up of death as everywhere else I have been, but here it is different, more individual. It's like thousands of minuscule stones all collected together. The water makes the tiny pieces seem to coagulate like one melted material.

"It's called sand," Disha says, standing on a hill a little ways inland, "The entire registana is covered in it. There isn't much water though, so I've never seen it this wet before."

"I like it," I say, "it's weird, you can feel it between your toes."

Disha laughs, "Yes, you can, but be careful. It is still death after all. You generally don't want to be in it much."

She is of course right, so I walk inland and up the hill where she stands. From here I can see much of the island. There are strange trees, unlike the ones in my forests before. These have only a few long, wide leaves and overlapping layers of bark going up the trunk. There are plants all along the ground, growing out of the death in very large supply. The plants are all very brightly colored in greens and yellows, and there are so many of them that I can't even see the ground they grew out of. There are birds of every color flying everywhere, each looking distinctly different.

Peri

In the center of the island is a very high hill that comes to a flat point at the top. This hill is higher than any I have seen before, so high that there is no grass or other plants growing on it from about halfway up to the very top. The hill is made of the dark grey stone of the walls.

And that's the strangest thing to me, there are no walls here. I look out at the horizon and the sky seems to go on forever and ever until it finally meets with the water that also seems infinite. Sky and water blend at some point that is difficult for me to tell since they are both the same brilliant blue. I can hardly believe just how far out it all goes, never seeming to really end, just going until I can't see it anymore.

"It's... huge." I say, "It just goes on forever."

"Yes," Disha replies, "It's amazing, I've never seen anything so big before in my life." We both marvel at the strange beauty of the immense water and sky.

"Ocean." I say.

"What?" Disha asks, turning to me.

"Ocean." I say again, "This water, it's called an ocean."

"How do you know?" Disha asks, "I thought you'd never seen one before."

I turn to the girl. "I haven't, but ocean is its name. I just know, that's it."

"Alright then," she says, "this will be our ocean."

We both smile, looking at each other, "Well," I say, "if that is our ocean, then I guess this is our island. I think we should explore it."

Disha laughs, "That sounds like a good idea," and so we depart, exploring the island we now have to ourselves.

In many ways the island is like my glade. The death makes up the ground throughout the island, and every now and then I find the same kind of grass or bush as I had before. Occasionally Disha would recognize a plant or bug from her registana as well. She would try to teach me her names for them, but like registana it was difficult in my mouth, and sometimes I would come up with my own name for things.

There is a spiny green plant with a milk you could eat I call a "cactus," Disha says they grew fairly commonly in the registana, and we see quite a few of them here as well. You have to be careful with these I find when I move to grab one. The spines on a cactus stab into your hands and get stuck there. Disha laughs a bit when I give a startled cry. "You can't grab it!" she says.

"Yeah," I say, trying to pull the spikes out of the palm of my hand, "I picked up on that."

She points out a small animal that is scuttling across some rocks. The animal is black and has a long tail with a spine at the end. Disha pulls me back when she sees it.

"Don't worry," I say, "I'm not too eager to touch things just now."

"That's a bicchu!" She says. "They are very poisonous, they will kill you if they sting you."

"Scorpion," I say, "it's a scorpion."

"Well, whatever you want to call it," Disha says, eyeing the small animal, "just stay away from it. They are very dangerous."

"Okay then," I say, "no grabbing the cactus plants, no getting near scorpions. I'm loving this island so far, so welcoming."

Disha laughs at that, easing up for the first time since we'd seen the scorpion. We continue to explore the island, making ourselves familiar with the layout of the land for everything but the hill, which we decide to leave for another day.

After many hours of exploration, we both scavenge around for some food to make a small meal between the two of us. The sun is constantly just above causing everything to feel especially hot. After eating we make a small shelter out of the large leaves from the trees around to get out of the sun then decide to sleep for a little while and regain our strength.

And so did I first meet Disha and we found our little island.

VIII

We make it our goal to explore the entirety of the island to see if we can find any other people and if there was an obvious way out. We also want to see if there are any notes on the island giving some direction. The only obvious place to look is on the hill in the center of the island.

Disha thinks it's dangerous to climb the mountain. She's worried that if we fell we'd die and the death would take us over. I am more concerned because halfway up where the plants no longer grew the sun would be beating down on the rock, and I am sure it must create an oven on the dark stone. If that happens, there's no way we could climb up its surface and see what's on top.

Even with both of these risks however I know we have to get to the top. I suggest we wait until clouds cover the sky for the water to fall, and so we focus our efforts on making a more stable structure to live in. We find two trees a few feet apart where we take a rope made of a long, thin leafed plant woven together and tie it between the two trunks. We make a netting out of more of the ropes running down to the ground from the rope. We take the larger leaves and position them between the ropes to make a more solid wall and roof. When it does rain, we will be able to keep out of it.

We also discover a thing called fire one day. The sun was beating down as normal, causing everything to feel especially hot. There were some leaves that had fallen from the trees and dried out in the heat, and when the sun continued to look down on them, something gray and wispy began to rise up from them. Soon an orange glowing substance began to eat away at the leaves, and when it got through the leaves only a black powder was left.

We found this orange substance appearing more and more, though only ever on the hot days. Usually it only affected the dry leaves that had fallen to the ground. I called the orange stuff "fire" and tried to conduct experiments on it as I did the death. The fire is somehow brought on by heat, and is very hot itself, but it doesn't have to be heat from the sun. I find that if two objects are rubbed together very quickly, they heat up in the same way they did if they sat in the sun. In this way, if two sticks are rubbed together quickly enough, they will begin sending out the gray wisps (which I call smoke) and if they're surrounded by the dry leaves, they make a fire.

Disha and I use fires all the time. If it's cold at night to give us some warmth, or sometimes we'll hold our food over a fire until it gets crispier and warm. We've tried many different foods this way, and found some that taste completely different when cooked this way. Nowadays cold food is a thing of the past, and we eat everything over a fire. This has become my favorite time of the day, when we sit over the fire and talk about where we've lived before. We compare notes on life and how we think it all works.

Disha asks me if I know what happens if you die, if I know of what world the death takes you to. I've never thought of anything like that, but I figure it is possible enough. If we can jump into pitch black holes and wind up on islands or go through tunnels into glades, then why couldn't there be an entire world below the death? I tell Disha this and she seems to agree with me. She asked if I think the life after you die is better.

I know the answer to this question. No, of course not. I remember again the gray man who died in front of me, and the terror he felt when the death had taken him over. I think about how the death once tried to take me when I had eaten the mushrooms. I think about all the pain and fear I had felt when that had happened. Surely nothing happy or good can come from something so terrifying and hurtful. I explain this to the girl but this time she doesn't seem as eager to agree with me.

"Why can't something good come from pain?" she asks me.

"Because pain means the death is coming, and then you die. Pain hurts, it doesn't feel good, it just keeps hurting even more." I reply.

Disha thinks about this for a moment, "Do you remember how we came here?" she asks me. "Your friends all disappeared, your home was destroyed, you lost everything. And then we met and we came here. Maybe it's not everything the glade was, but is it all that bad? Even if you felt all that pain to get here and had to lose everything, we gained something else."

I nod at her, "I suppose that's true," I say, though it isn't. I haven't really lost everything. I still haven't told Disha about him, but my best friend, the man in the water has indeed made it here with me. I had first seen him in the ocean and some of the ponds or puddles strewn throughout the island. At first he was very excited to see me, as I him, but we were also both concerned. I haven't told my new friend about my old one, I don't know what she would think of him.

We know we should tell Disha soon, maybe she'd even like the man in the water, but we keep putting it off, always planning to tell her at some point but never actually getting around to it. She of course doesn't ask about him. She has no reason to, though she gives me strange stares whenever she finds me looking into the water for a long time.

I usually laugh it off if she does find me, say I was just remembering my time in the glade. This isn't entirely a lie, as that's what the man in the water and I mostly talk about. I also tell him about Disha and the things we talk about together. He seems very interested in her, always listening with rapture even though he obviously knew about her enough to tell about her at the same moment. I find it nice being able to talk with someone who understands me so well. Disha is fun to talk to, but she had lived in a completely different place than I had, whereas the man in the water has been with me since the beginning.

I make a small bowl out of a round, hard, brown fruit that grew on the trees. I fill the bowl with water and keep it near me when I sleep. I can always look over and see the man in the water checking back on me, and it comforts me to have something familiar in a place that's so foreign. I try to hide the bowl from Disha, and it remains another secret between the man and I.

We wait out the days in this way, living under the sun, enjoying our make-shift house, talking to each other over meals of edible plants. It's not a bad time, but we still haven't managed to get up the mountain. I'm sitting on the shore, talking to the man in the water, when we both look toward the sky. There, in the center of the clear blue sky, just over the sun, is a single black cloud.

I run back to the shelter, calling for Disha. She isn't there, and so I tear through the island looking for her as the sky continues to grow darker. I find her after around ten minutes picking some berries off a small bush. She turns questioningly when she hears her name and I point up at the sky. Looking up I see her face suddenly lift into a smile.

"To the mountain?" she asks.

"To the mountain!" I reply smiling, then we turn to the center of the island and start running up the slope.

"How long do you think we have before it begins raining down on us?" she asks.

"Maybe thirty minutes," I say as a loud peal of thunder roars from above. I slow for just a moment as fear grips my heart. I have never managed to get used to the noise from the sky, and I have to force myself to continue moving upwards.

Soon we're at the proper base of the mountain, and it becomes easier to climb on all fours than with just our legs. We are soon grasping at the plants growing on the side of the mountain to pull ourselves up, and shortly after this we find that the death is no longer the source of the plants. They now grow out of the rock that previously made up the walls.

I reach out and touch the rock, confirming with a glowing handprint that it is indeed the same material. This means we are getting much higher on the mountain than I thought could have been possible in so short a time.

"Wait," I tell Disha as another peal of thunder roars from above.

We sit there, clinging to plants on the side of the wall, when I realize we're still moving upward. The plants themselves are gliding up the face of the rock wall in the same way that the wall had moved along the ground in the glade. As we cling to the plants we're brought up higher and higher.

I look to Disha and see that she has noticed this as well. We're both hopeful as this means we are that much closer to the top of the mountain. We begin laughing at how much easier this will now be as we coast up the side of the wall. Then another peal of thunder roars, and it seems to shake the mountain itself. Looking up at the wall I can see that we have now reached the point where the plants begin to thin out, and they will soon disappear entirely.

What this means occurs to me a second before I felt the plants I was grasping begin to grow smaller and smaller, shrinking into the dark stone of the mountain. Then they sink fully into the rock. Disha and I have one quick second to look at one another before we are falling.

We fall down the mountain, rolling down over and over again, crashing into bushes, trees, and rocks as we fall all the way down back to the base of the mountain as the rain begins to pour and congeal with the death to place us in a muddy pit.

And there we sit until the rain stops, until the thunder stops its roaring, until everything stops spinning and the light stops shining and we both pass into a blackness that takes us over forever.

When I wake up, I'm half buried in mud that has fallen down the mountain. Looking to my right I can see Disha in a similar position, though she's still unconscious. I stand up, letting mud slop to the ground as I look around. I can now see that this has been no ordinary storm. Trees everywhere have fallen and lay around the island precariously, many bushes have been uprooted and thrown about, and the death-mud covers everything.

As I look out at all the damage done, I feel a sudden pain in my head, as though I have been stabbed through the center of my skull. I grab at my head and cry out, but the pain remains. I continue crying out as my head feels ready to split apart. My noise rouses Disha and she is soon up and holding me as I curl into a ball and weep while my brain is torn to shreds.

We remain that way for what may have been hours or seconds, I've lost all concept of time. Finally the pain seems to ebb away just enough for me to stop crying and screaming and sit up. I remain silent for a few minutes more before Disha quietly speaks.

"Are... are you all right?" she asks almost inaudibly.

I think about that question. Am I okay? The world I have come to call my new home is torn apart. I have no understanding for how my world truly works and yet I'm always frightened by how it exists, and now some unseen threat seems to be dominating my mind. It's as though the universe has set out to restrain me from learning too much about my surroundings. "I don't know," I finally answer, "but my head hurts."

Disha gingerly takes my head in her hands and examines it for any sign of cuts or breaks, but she finds nothing. "Where exactly does it hurt?" she asks.

"I don't know exactly, around this area," I say as I carefully point to the top of my head. Pressing just a little harder though, I feel no more pain than before. I continue feeling around my skull for any sign of what could cause the pain I had been feeling. "Do you see anything at all?" I ask.

"Nothing," the girl replies. "I don't know what caused your attack, but I don't think it was any physical injury. Let's get you back to the tent and let you sleep."

"I've been sleeping for hours," I say, trying to wave her off as I stood again.

"You've been passed out, that's not the same thing," she says, ignoring my hands and catching me as I fall in a limp I didn't known I had.

"Fine," I say, "you can help me, just don't keep looking at me like that. It's just a headache. Not like I've lost my entire arm or something." My point would have been made a lot more believably if I didn't step into a hole with my limp and shriek out as I fall at just that moment.

Disha laughs as I again fall against her and smiles while she helps me up. "Oh ,forgive me," she says, her smile all too audible, "I didn't realize you were so well along." Despite the ridiculous situation she attempts to hold back her laughter and for the rest of our slow walk she keeps to herself.

When we do get back to the tent she again examines my head but still finds nothing. She leaves me alone while she goes to find some food for the both of us. Lying alone in the tent, I try to get some rest and recover a bit from my apparent injuries that have no real source. Try as I might though, I cannot get my body to shut down.

I'm worried when it comes down to it, about the island and the damage the storm must have caused, about whatever's happened to my head that's causing it to hurt so much, and about the fact that I don't think I'm going to be able to get up the mountain. I don't know what's up there, but I know it is vital to finding my way off this island, and this island will not be my home forever. I have to get off of it, and I will do whatever I need to badget to the top of that mountain if that's what getting off takes.

I wonder if Disha is as resolved about getting off this island as I am. She hadn't had a home before like I had, so maybe she doesn't mind the island. Compared to her stories of the registana this island is paradise, and I can't imagine she wants to go back to where she had come from. But I'm not from the registana, I had had a home, and I have a purpose. I am not going to let death win over me, and I am not going to lose my home.

I don't just mean the glade. I mean the safety and familiarity I felt with it. I knew how the glade worked, I knew what happened when, who was there, and what they did. I have determined that I will have that again, and it is as much a priority to me as conquering death. There has to be a place, somewhere, where I will be safe, even if that means I heave to create such a place myself. I won't simply be beaten by the world and its little rules.

I keep all of these things in mind as blackness creeps into the corners of my vision and I soon fall fast asleep.

IX

I sleep for a long time, but I have no way of knowing how long for sure. When I do wake Disha is sitting quietly in the corner weaving some of the longer leaves into a bowl shape. Near by there is a pile of fruits and vegetables she must have scavenged while I have been sleeping. I lie there, silent for a moment as I watch her. Her hands move gracefully with the leaves, in and out, over and under as the basket takes form between her fingers.

I'm just about to speak out when she suddenly looks to her right and gets up, dashing out of the tent to some unknown focus. I consider simply drifting back off to sleep, when I notice my brown bowl sitting just above my head. There's no way it could have survived the storm, the tent itself is ragged and torn after going through the ordeal. I wonder how the bowl could have gotten here, and determine it could only have been Disha that placed it there.

I feel very badly about this. The bowl is the medium through which I have been keeping secrets from the girl, and here she is unknowingly aiding me in keeping them. I'm not surprised she has noticed how I keep the bowl nearby, she probably just thinks it's in case I grow thirsty. The reality is I simply don't trust her when it comes to the man in the water.

I sit up enough to look into the bowl, and there I see my old friend. He looks a bit ragged, as though he's been having just as bad a time as I have these past hours since the storm started. I give him a small smile and ask how he's been. Something is wrong. What is it? Something seems off. It's almost as if-

Wait, that's it. When I asked the man in the water, he hadn't asked back. I sit there marveling at this strange phenomenon, and see the man looks just as bewildered. "Did you..." I ask, but stop when I hear the same words directed back to me. I must be dreaming or imagining things, the man hadn't moved independently, he never does. We are always in perfect rhythm.

Sometimes I had almost wondered if we were the same person, as close as we seem in mind and motion.

Yes, we are the same, he had asked me how I was too, I'm simply so out of it I hadn't noticed. I rub my head again and lie back down. I must have really hit it for so this to have happened. I'm losing my grip on sanity.

Just as I'm contemplating this thought, Disha walks back into the tent and surveys me. She smiles when she sees I'm awake, then goes to the food in the corner. Using her basket that she must have finished while she was gone, she gathered some round yellow fruits and other foods and gives them to me as a meal. I sit up and offer a broken thank you as I take the basket.

I take one of the large yellow fruits and roll it around in my hand before taking a bite. It's extremely juicy and the liquids runs down my chin as I bite into the meat of the plant. It tastes excellent but unfamiliar to me. "What is this stuff?" I ask, "I don't recognize it. Where did you find it?"

"It was growing on a tree a little ways off. I've never seen any tree like it, but the fruit on it looked good. I tried a little and, as you can now attest, it was delicious, so I picked all of the ripe ones I saw. It's one of the few trees still standing and holding its fruit. Nearly all of them fell down."

"Yeah, it looked pretty nasty," I say and then finish the fruit in my hand. Looking in the basket, I now realize I recognize few of the fruits here, Disha had found all sorts of plants I had never seen. "How far did you have to go to get all of these?"

"Not too far, believe it or not. Everything was within a hundred feet or so of our tent."

I look up at the girl, berries filling my mouth, "That's impossible, I've never seen most of this stuff. How could I have missed all of this? I mean the plants grow wild around here but not that wild, I'd still notice some of this stuff." Holding up a small, strangely shaped fruit no larger than my curled up finger I look at her questioningly.

"That's what I thought," she says, "but they're there. I don't know, maybe the storm just moved some things around so we could see it."

"Yeah, maybe," I mutter, but I don't believe it, and looking at Disha's eyes I can see she doesn't really either. But, this food is indeed delicious and so long as we can find it neither of us is particularly interested in questioning how it got there. I finish up the meal and look back at Disha, who is already working on another basket. She can see that I had finished the fruit.

"So," she says, "how's about we explore what's changed since the rain?"

"Sure," I say and stand up to leave the tent with her. "Anything in particular that's new?"

"Besides the trees I haven't noticed anything," the girl says without turning around, "but I haven't had too much time to go looking either. I was waiting for you to wake up first." She stands just outside the tent, hands on her hips, as she looks out over the island. Looking myself I can see that the destruction was no better than before, so I hadn't imagined that. But, now that I'm looking, I can indeed see a few exotic trees spread here and there, all quite close by, holding every kind of fruit that Disha had provided me with.

"Well," I say, "let's get on with it then." And with this, I start off in a direction to the right of the tent, limping as I try to hurry off.

"Oh, I forgot, I made this for you too," Disha says. Then she ducks behind the tent and comes back with a large stick. "It's for your limp," she says as she hands me the staff. Taking it in my hand I see that it had been rubbed down at one section for a handhold. It is just the right size and strength without being too heavy.

"It's excellent," I say, "thank you." Then I look up at her and smile, "Really, thank you very much."

"It's no problem, I just didn't want you to have too hard a time of it while you were healing. It's not much, but it should help."

"It will," I say as I test it out. And so we walk out together.

All over the island there are changes to the landscape from before. There had once been a spot with two standing stones leaning against each other to form a sort of natural archway. However, when we walk to the location where the arch should have been, all we can see are cactus plants growing out of completely flat and cleared death. Many of the trees that had been memorable for one reason or another have also disappeared into nowhere. Many rough or overgrown areas are now flat, and many are just patches of death without any plants, looking like a gross bald spot on the surface of the world.

Continuing on we find cliffs over the ocean where the gray sandy beaches had been before. Deep cracks run though the land, falling down hundreds of feet into pure blackness beyond what we can see. We even find a few places where rocks and boulders have been shaken from some place up on the mountain, but when we look up we can see no sign of where they may have fallen from.

"It's so different," Disha whispers as we looked up the face of the mountain.

"I know," I reply, "it's like an entirely new island. The only thing that's the same is this stupid mountain." I punctuate this last sentence by using my staff to hurl a rock at the wall. That's another change, the plants that had been growing halfway up the peak are now all gone too. Now the mountain looks like an ugly pillar thrusting out to grasp the sun that sits still in the center of the sky, shining down and cooking everything beneath it.

Disha takes a few steps to the mountain's face, then takes her hand and places it against the bare stone. I see a light begin to shine beneath her palm, but my mouth drops when I see that it isn't blue, but a reddish color. She laughs when she sees my face.

"What," she asks, "you didn't think you were the only one that could draw on walls did you?"

"No, no" I stutter, "I'm just surprised that your light is different, it's red. Mine is always blue." And with that I stumble forward on my staff and place my own hand next to her glowing print.

The girl stifles her laugh a bit then says, "Well come on, Peri, we're completely different people who have experienced different things. Did you think everyone's mark on the world is the same?"

I think about that. Does that mean that every person's mark was just a little bit different? I think about how I made the notes with the glowing signs, the advice I gave through it to some unknown person. I had never seen my notes for long before they whisked away into the sky. Were they awfully different from the notes I had received? If our experiences and differences define who we are, does that mean that the advice we give will be shown differently each time? I wonder what would happen if I compared a note I wrote to one Disha did, if I'm right, they would probably be entirely different.

"You're right I guess," I mutter, pulling out of my thoughts. "I guess I've just never actually seen you draw on the walls, so I was surprised is all." I sigh and look up the mountain's face. "Too bad we can't just draw our way up this thing, It'd get us up easily enough if that were the case."

Disha offers a wry laugh. "What if we're supposed to go down the holes in the island, the one's that weren't there before the storm? What if that's the exit?"

"Maybe," I say. The truth is I'd already considered the possibility, but I just don't believe it. For one thing it's too similar to how we had gotten out of the glad when it was destroyed, and I feel like this should be different somehow. I can't explain it well, but shouldn't we be moving forward? Not just repeating the same ideas again and again? I feel like different points in life call for different approaches.

And beside all this, I still feel strongly that we need to scale this mountain. Maybe it's just idle curiosity, but I really need to get to that peak and see what is up there. It's something new, something different, I know it, and there has to be a way to get up there. Obviously climbing is out of the question, there aren't even plants on the mountain face to cling to anymore. If there were some way to attach steps to the stone then we could just walk up, but I have never seen the dark stones dent, neither here nor in the glade or the valley before that. No, the only time these walls ever seemed to change at all was when they opened into tunnels or were pressed upon with skin, causing the glow.

"Hello there," Disha says, shifting so she was in direct eyesight. "Hey! You with me here Peri?"

I laugh and scratch my head, "Sorry, just lost in thought I guess."

"Guess you hurt your head worse than we thought," the girl teases. "Hey, maybe you can just daydream your way into a new world. We can save all that climbing time, especially since it doesn't take you more than a moment to move a million miles away."

"Haha very funny," I say in mock offense. I drop my staff to the ground and sit down, lying down on the base of the mountain. I close my eyes against the sun and am just getting comfortable when I smell fire. There's no fire here, we haven't brought any with us, where is the smell coming from?

I open my eyes and see smoke coming up from either side of my head, and that's when I start to feel the heat at the base of my skull. I scream and spring forward at least five feet, grabbing the back of my head and trying to put out whatever fire had started there, but I don't feel anything. I spin around and see a very bright imprint of the back of my head glowing out of the gray stone I had been leaning on.

Stupid stupid stupid **stupid** *stupid* **STUPID**! I know not to come into direct contact with the stone! Really this was the first thing I learned when I had woken up in the cave at the beginning of my life. It is common sense!

I would have continued yelling at myself in my head if I didn't hear Disha snort behind me. I spin around and see her clutching her mouth with both hands, her eyes positioned in an obvious smile. When I make eye contact she loses control and begins roaring with laughter. Soon I feel my face burning far more than my hair.

She remains in this position for what feels like hours. "Okay Disha," I finally say, a little annoyed but more embarrassed, "I think we both get it. It was funny, let's move on."

She looks at me and laughs again but then makes an honest effort to muffle her hysterics. "Now then," I say, "can you please check my hair and make sure nothing is wrong, it was smoking quite a bit."

"On that point we agree," she says, chuckling again. Then she walks behind me and began sifting through my hair. "This is weird," she says.

"That is not a particularly comforting thing to say after someone's hair has been burning," I joke. "You should work on your bedside manner."

Disha laughs, "No, that's not what I mean. There aren't any problems here. I saw it smoking too, but there's no hair missing, and nothing's burned up."

"Huh," I say, "that is weird." I'm just about to write this off as some freak tendency testifying to the power of my hair when my eyes light up with an idea. The hair doesn't burn up, but it did cause a glow on the stone as much as my actual skin. I wonder if this means...

I run over to the circle of blue glowing stone and run my hand across it. "Um," Disha says from behind me, "now forgive me if I'm wrong, I'm sure you totally know what you're doing and all, but I would think that nearly burning off your head would lead you to exert some caution when it comes to touching that stone with your bare skin again. Ya know, just trying to keep you from killing yourself and all that."

I ignore her and continue feeling along the stone here. A smile creeps up my face as I feel what I am hoping for. "Disha, come here, give me your hand." Disha raises one eyebrow but comes over and kneels down next to me. She offers her hand and I place it carefully against the glowing stone. The light begins to turn purple where she touches but otherwise no difference is made. The girl looks at me questioningly.

"Other than my hand heating up, am I supposed to be noticing anything?" she asks.

I smile at her, "Run your hand from the outer edge of the glow to the inside, feel any difference?"

She looks doubtful, but does what I ask. "I still don't feel anything, what am I looking for?"

My smile grows wider, "Disha, it dips."

Disha looks back at me, eyes widening as her mouth bursts open into a smile. She jumps up and screams as I stumble to my feet with my staff. We quickly gather all the food we can find and throw a small party feast for the two of us in celebration of this brilliant truth. Then we dance for hours.

No, we don't.

That is a lie.

In reality, Disha continues looking very confused and raises her eyebrows as she slowly says, "Peri, are you okay? Do you need to go get some more sleep?"

I laugh, "No, I'm fine, really! Think about it though, the stone dips where the hair touched it, and the hair wasn't burned." I pluck a hair from my head and drop it on the stone. I wait a moment, and then see what I'd hoped, a light blue glow begins to emanate from underneath the hair. "Disha, look, the hair will make the glow on the stone, and if it stays there long enough, it will begin pushing into the rock wall itself, meaning that we can make holes in the stone."

Half a second later Disha's eyes actually do begin to widen as the wheels in her head whir and figure out what I'm saying. "Then, we can…"

"We can make steps in the wall! We can climb up!" I shout.

Disha smiles, now fully realizing what I was saying. "We could be up to the top in just a few hours!"

"Exactly!" I squeal, "It'll just take a little bit of preparation, we're practically already at the top."

Disha laughs at my enthusiasm, "Well calm down, we're not there yet. Let's go back to the tent and gather all the supplies we need and get some sleep. There's no rush, it's not exactly like we've got someplace to be. Let's just take it one step at a time."

I laugh and nod, beginning to walk back to camp with her. She's right, we need to take our time, but she's wrong about something else. I do have someplace to be. Home, and I'm gonna get there. As we're walking I'm struck with a ridiculous idea and turn to Disha, "One might almost say that we're gonna draw our way up the mountain." We both laugh and walk on, not even noticing that the sun has moved downwards a nearly imperceptible amount.

X

When we get back to camp we grab the baskets Disha made and start collecting food from the surrounding landscape. I'm careful to pick quite a few of the large yellow fruits as they're firm, taste delicious, and fill you up well, meaning they're perfect for a long climb. I also forage around for nuts and some smaller fruits, some of which are strange to me but that I decide are worth trying. When I just begin to think about heading back I can see it's a solid amount of food, at least for myself.

I can see that Disha's basket is also nearly bursting with the amount of food she has packed into it. We gather some more items, then take both baskets to the tent where we lie out the spread. There's such an abundance of food that I'm sure it will last forever, I have never collected so many fruits and nuts in one place.

"We should cook and dry out some of these," Disha says, "They'll last longer that way."

She's right, we had noticed that if fruit was broken into smaller pieces and left on a warm surface, like a stone under the sun or over a fire, it will shrivel up and last far longer than fruit normally will. It also changes the flavor, and while I don't particularly like the taste it brought on when dried, it was at least different, and after eating the same foods again and again for weeks diversity was always sorely desired.

We then take about a third of the fruits and break them into smaller pieces to dry out on a large flat rock about ten feet from the tent. We take another third and cook them so they're a little crispy. These won't last as long as the dried fruits, but they'll go far longer than raw. The last third we just leave raw. The plan is to eat the raw foods first, then the cooked ones, and lastly the dried provisions after we had finished all other fare. In this way we'll have food for the longest period of time.

When we finish we smile and look at all the food we now have in our possession, and how efficiently we have processed it. "There's only one problem," I say as we look out at the edible layout.

"What's that?" the girl asks.

"We have all this food," I answer, "but it's not as though we can hold it in our hands when we're climbing the steeper portions of the mountain. We need to find some way of carrying it all without the use of our hands or arms."

We think about it a moment, when Disha says, "I could weave baskets, and add a strap made from rope to it so that we could put the food into the bag and wear it over our shoulder."

"Could you make something like that?" I ask. "Without it breaking?"

"I don't know," the girl says, "but it's worth a shot. There's not much else I can think of that would work."

"I guess you're right. Well, while you figure that out I'm gonna go try and see if there's some way we can get the hair from our heads without ripping it out of our skulls."

Disha laughs and goes to gather leaves. I sit in a corner of the tent and rack my brain. I pluck another hair from my head and look at it. I haven't given much thought to hair in the past, it was just a part of my body, and it's not as though I give an abundance of thought to my legs or nose. They all have a purpose, and they serve it, I usually don't have to understand them to make use of them.

But now I have a new use and need for my hair, and I need to know some more about it to accomplish my plan. I pull the strand between my two hands. It's surprisingly resilient but still breaks in two after sufficient force is applied. If there is some way I can break it or cut it I can save myself the pain and harm of pulling. The problem is, I don't have anything sharp enough to cut the hair. I would have to make something somehow, and I can think of only one way to do so.

I run out to the mountain's base and look around for a small, long stone. I hunt for a few minutes before my efforts are rewarded with the perfect candidate for my plan. I hurry back to the tent with it in my hand with a handle of death, the same way I held my torch, and take the hair I had plucked. I pull a few more strands of hair from my head and braid the hair together to form a small cord. Then I use this cord against the stone to melt it down.

In the same way that I plan on getting up the mountain, I make my knife. I use the hair cord to burn the stone down to a wedge that is thin and very sharp. I run my finger against the brightly glowing blade and accidentally slice the skin. The death begins to sizzle and bubble up with my blood dripping down my hand onto the blade before falling to the ground. I stick my finger into my mouth to stop the bleeding and keep any more blood dripping onto the ground. The last thing I want now, when everything seems to finally be going right, was for the death to get hungry and start jumping out to grab me.

I set the knife down next to me and wait for Disha to come back. After a little while, she walks back to the tent, her hands full of leaves. She sits down and begins to weave the leaves in the pattern she had invented and eyes the brightly glowing knife on the floor.

"What is that for?" she asks, "Another torch?"

I shake my head, "No, this is a knife, I made it so we can cut our hair to use on the mountain."

"Does it work?"

"I don't know yet. It's really sharp," I show her the cut on the tip of my finger, "I'd rather not get that thing close to my head when I can't seem where it's going. I figure we can cut each other's hair."

"Well, that would be a good plan," she says, "but then I'd have to let you hold a very sharp object in direct proximity to my head, and I'm just not sure I can risk that much."

"Oh shut up," I say, but smiles break out across our faces after holding the mock intense stare for all of about two seconds. Disha continues weaving while I take up the knife and move behind her. I take up as much of her hair as I can without pulling too hard and place the knife just above my hand. I apply a little more pressure when immediately both Disha and I spin around as we hear a screaming, moaning sound growing louder and louder from inland. The cry grows so loud we soon have to cover our ears and I drop the knife on the ground as we both run out of the tent to find the source of this pandemonium.

At first we can see nothing, just the mountain and plants making up the island. Then we see a figure running directly toward us at speeds I didn't even know were possible. My blood turns to ice when I see the man better as he gets closer. The man's skin and clothing are all made of a single dark gray color. It is another man of stone.

I remember the first one I had seen, back in the valley I had first come to, back when I didn't know what the death was. As I'm remembering all of this, I see what looks like a flood of death rising up like a tidal wave behind the man.

Coming straight for us.

Disha and I immediately run in opposite directions, still covering our ears as the man screams out louder than anything I had ever experienced. My limp slows me down tremendously and I have forgotten my staff, but I waddle as far as I can quick as my dead leg will allow me. Looking at the wave of pale gray death I know there is no way I will be able to escape it, it's going to catch me as soon as it reaches me.

The man is now only about ten feet away, the wave another fifteen behind him. Just as I'm sure he'll pass me and cause the wave of death to take me up in its rumbling charge, the man jumps into the air higher than anything I have ever seen and two appendages appear from his back.

They are *wings. Like birds have!*

My jaw drops as he does quite the opposite, spinning higher into the air as his wings beat at the air below him. The wave of death immediately changes directions and instead of rushing towards me it shoots into the air, a beacon of death, a testament to the relentlessness of the cold, moist substance.

The winged man and his gray, formless pursuer fly another few hundred feet into the air until the man is nearly invisible. Then they again change direction and rush back inland toward the mountain. I watch as the man flies closer and closer to the peak and then slew right into the top of it from above. I can't see where he has gone, but the vast amount of death rushes down into the mountain's head as well.

It continues seemingly pouring itself into some unseen hole or other on the top of the mountain's peak. After a few dozen seconds the death parts from the ground and flows into the mountain, cutting off its supply but still apparently pursuing the man.

Or maybe it isn't, maybe that's why it's stopped.

Regardless I don't waste my time thinking about it too long. I have to find Disha and make sure she is okay. I run back to the tent and soon see her running back from the opposite direction. She looks breathless but otherwise okay. I hold out a thumbs up to verify this and happily see her flash the sign back at me. Then we both enter the tent and collapse against the ground, panting heavily.

"What was that thing?" Disha asks when she has caught her breath.

"I don't know," I say, "but it's not the first time I've seen one. In my first home, before I lived in the glade, there was a valley I came too. I saw a man like him there, he died. But he didn't have wings, I've never seen anything like that!"

"Me neither," Disha says, "and I've never seen the death so aggressive. Where do you think they went?"

"No idea, but it looked like they actually went into the mountaintop itself. Is that possible?"

"You're asking the wrong person Peri. I'd never even seen a mountain till I came here. I'm not exactly an expert on them. It could have a hole though, I guess. I mean that's why you want to get up there right? To find some door or something?"

"I'm not sure just why I want to get up there, I just know I do and I will." I glance into the bowl of water nearby, the man in the water looks as concerned as I do. Just as I'm glancing away, I see him look towards the mountain, a look of worry in his eyes. I nearly scream when I see him act independently for this, the second time, but manage to hold my tongue so as to not alert Disha that something is wrong. Thankfully though, she's still occupied in the stone man and the mountain to even be looking at me.

"We should get back to work preparing to get up the mountain," I say. "Where were we?"

"I believe," Disha says, the slightest smile creeping back onto her look of concern, "that you were in the middle of using that knife to cut my head off."

"I was not! I was just cutting your hair!" I yell.

"Oh, and that's why my hair is so neatly cut and your knife 'slipped' to nearly slice my neck in two," she points at her hair that remains thoroughly uncut.

"Well, sure," I reply, "just blame *me* for the crazy bird man with a tsunami of death chasing on his heels straight for us."

Disha's smile grows wider and she starts laughing, "I'm *glad* the bird man did arrive! Otherwise your dastardly plan would have been accomplished and I may well be dead!"

I glare at the girl across the tent. "Well, fine then," I say, "if I'm such a villain, maybe you should cut *my* hair first." And with this I offer her the blade.

"Maybe I should," she says, eyes sparkling with amusement.

"Don't move too much, I may just *accidentally* slice off an ear or two."

"I don't like the way you say, 'accidentally.'"

"Careful there," Disha says, "that whole head of yours moves when you talk. Wouldn't want it to move anywhere it shouldn't now would we?"

"Oh just cut it already," I say, but now I'm smiling too. I've never had these sorts of humorous banters with my friends in the glade or the man in the water, and it's fun to test who can keep the joke up longer.

I feel Disha pull up all my hair and press the knife against it. Then she slices once and cuts through some of the bundle. It's a strange feeling, like weight being relieved from my head so much so that it almost falls forward. Disha continues running the knife back and forth until all the hair has been severed. I run my fingers through the hair now no more than a tenth its original length. I can feel my scalp and the air seemed colder all around me. I shudder once and drop my hand.

"Did it hurt?" Disha asks.

"No, don't worry. You don't feel a thing, it is kind of a weird feeling though."

"Wait, how can it feel weird if you can't feel anything?"

I blink, not sure how to answer her. This was a legitimately good question. I hadn't felt anything, but I had at the same time. "It doesn't matter," I say, no answer forthcoming in my mind. "It's your turn now. Don't worry, the only way you'd feel pain is if I slip and cut your skin."

"So then it's pretty much guaranteed I'll get hurt then?" she teases.

"Haha, you're oh so funny, now come on." I take the knife as Disha and I switch places. I again take up her hair in my hand and mark the spot I will cut just a little above where I grip the handful. I quickly slice through the threadlike strands and hold the girl's hair in my hand, no longer attached to her head. Disha begins running her hand through the small tuft of hair still clutching her head in the same way I had.

"It's cold," she says.

"I know, I hope we get used to it. I don't particularly want to go through life shivering and feeling off balance."

"So, what else do we have to do to get ready?"

"I figure I'd attach the hair around two sticks, so we can both burn grips and footsteps into the mountain at the same time without using our hands. You still need to finish the bags, and then we need to make some sort of protection for our hands so they don't have to come into direct contact with the stone face of the mountain."

"I think I can make something like that," Disha says, and we again split into different projects.

XI

I'm sure I can attach the hair to the branches. All I'll need to do is find a sturdy stick of the right size and tie the hair around the top. It can't take more than ten minutes I'm sure. I go out to find the branches I need from the surrounding countryside, glad I'll be back in the tent resting up before the expedition within a few minutes. After the mysterious encounter with the stone man I don't want to take chances away from Disha.

I end up searching for what must be three hours before I *finally* find the second stick, the first I had found maybe an hour before. I'm shocked it took me so long to accomplish my goal, it would have been a snap in the glade. But, as evidenced in so many things, this is not the glade. Unlike there, most of the trees here don't actually have branches, just one long trunk all the way to the top. This means that finding branches proves a never ending quest with little reward. The branches I do find are from the trees that have been knocked down in the last storm, but even looking through these I have to be careful that the wood is strong enough to support the weight pushed against it without breaking, an even more rare find.

Eventually though I do procure the perfect candidates for my project, and I take them back to the tent. I then take the hair, mine first, and wrap it around the end of one of the branches. When I go to tie it however, the hair proves less than cooperative. It's difficult to get a handful on thousands of strands to act as a single rope, meaning that tying is immensely more difficult than it should be. The only way I can get it to do what I want is to tie smaller portions the whole bundle together, leading to about twenty knots arranged around the makeshift tool.

When I finish with the first one I look proudly at it, it wasn't as easy as I originally hoped or believed, but it is still just as good in the final product. I then take up the other branch and slowly tie

Disha's hair around the end in the same way I had mine.

Disha comes in a few minutes after I finish my project, two complete satchels made of the woven leaves over her shoulder. "All finished then?" she asks upon entering the tent.

"Yeah, but it took forever," I says.

"Oh I'm sure, and that's why you're just lying down here, probably napping. I bet you worked five minutes and have just been sitting around." Even as she says it I can see the gleam of humor in her eyes that means she's again teasing me, as she so often does.

"You know if you're always playing around like that, I may never know when you're actually being serious," I say.

"Who said anything about joking?" She gasps and puts her hand to her chest. "Certainly you don't think that I would ever lie or tease you. Oh not me, never!"

"Oh certainly not," I say grinning, but inside my emotions are far more mixed. Hearing Disha joke about lying when I'm still keeping the secret about the man in the water makes me feel awful. "Hey Disha," I mutter, "I need to tell you about something."

"Okay, but first let me show you what I made," Disha says, and then swings the two bags off her shoulder in front of me.

"These are really nice," I say holding one in my hands and feeling it over. The girl had somehow managed to weave the leaves so tightly that you can barely see where one leaf ends and another starts. It's easy to tell that these would prove amply strong enough to hold our food over the climb. Looking inside I see two strangely shaped objects covered in death mud. I must look surprised because Disha speaks up.

"They're for our hands, I call them gloves. We should be able to hold to the mountain's stop with them on." She takes one of the "gloves" from me and puts her hand into a large hole on one side. Then she fills the bag-like object with her fingers in five slots on the other end. She flexes her fingers, showing how the glove has full flexibility. I take one up myself and see that they're made of woven leaves like the baskets but with a coat of mud over the surface. I put two of them on and am surprised at just how comfortable they feel.

"These are excellent," I say while holding the two gloves over my hands. "How did you develop the pattern?"

"I don't know, just made it up I guess," Disha says modestly as her cheeks turn the colors of a particular fruit I had had in the glade I had called a strawberry. "It's a lot like the bowl but where you'd make the bottom you just split it into smaller bowls that go on for a long time like this," here she pulls out another glove prototype without the fingers finished. I can see the weaving a little better, but the precise workings are still strange and complex to my untrained eyes.

"That means nothing to me," I say laughing, "I'll simply have to settle for appreciating your skill in ignorance."

"Well," Disha says, "your ignorance is something I'm fairly used to by now."

"In that case," I say, "I'll just take my new tools and climb the mountain alone."

"As though you could."

"I could certainly try. It'd be far easier for me since I'll have the devices necessary for climbing."

"Hey there now, *my* hair, *my* tool."

"Fight ya for 'em."

"Let's go."

We both laugh and then I remember the man in the water. I'm going to do it, I *am* going to tell her. "Right, Disha, there's still something I need to talk to you about."

"What," Disha asks, obviously still playing around, "did you secretly choose a weaker stick for me so it will snap?"

"What? No!" I exclaim.

"Oh, so then you'll sabotage my bag I suppose and keep me from having any food, or maybe your plan is to punch holes in my gloves so I burn my hands."

"No, Disha! Listen, this is important!" I yell, trying to cut her off. It works, and Disha's face suddenly loses all sign of humor.

"Is something wrong?" she asks quietly.

I sigh, here we go. "Disha, there's a secret I've been keeping from you." Disha eyes me steadily, unsure of what I'd say. "I haven't traveled alone. Even before you I had someone who has stayed with me, ever since I was born into the valley I first lived in."

"And why have I never seen him if he's always been with you? I'm not dumb, Peri, my eyes do work."

"I know that, but it's a little more complicated than that. See, this person, this man, he doesn't exactly *live* in the same way we do."

"What does that even mean?" Disha demands, beginning to grow frustrated. I open my mouth to answer her question, but then decide the only way I can really explain it is to show the girl. I turn around and grab the bowl, bringing it to her.

"Look inside," I say, "what do you see?"

Disha looks into the bowl, but to my disappointment only says, "I see water, and the inside of a bowl. Um, is that some dust? There's some dust."

"What?" I ask, confused. I look into the bowl myself and am astounded to see only water. The man in the water has simply disappeared without a trace. "No, this can't be happening, he was here, he's always here. He's always around!"

"Your friend, was in the bowl?" Disha asks slowly.

"No of course not! He was in the water!" I shout back, louder than is probably necessary.

"Oh and I guess that makes perfect sense then," Disha says sarcastically, but this time there was no humor in her eyes.

"I'm not lying!" I yell at her, returning her smug look with a glare.

"Sure you're not. You're just wasting our time with your mythical friend who lives in the bowl."

"It's true!"

"Then where is he?"

"I don't know, but he's gotta be somewhere!"

I'm sure we would have continued yelling back and forth like this, probably rising in volume and possibly even coming to blows, if the ground itself didn't started vibrating. I can't say for certain exactly when it had started, but we both notice it now. The shaking is accompanied by a low rumbling noise coming from what seems to be the mountain.

We both run out of the tent, our quarrel forgotten for the moment, looking at the central pillar of the island. There is a deep, dark smoke coming from the top of the peak.

"That doesn't look good," I say in awe.

"Congratulations, that's the least stupid thing you've said all day," the girl replies.

"Oh shut up for a moment will you? What are we gonna do?"

"Well, obviously we're *not* climbing the mountain when it's like that."

This is a crucial moment, a moment when I have to make a decision. I can remain down here by the tent, accepting whatever life the island has to offer and probably dying at some point, or I can keep challenging death and make sure that I get out of here, by sheer determination if nothing else. "Maybe you're not, but I'm going." And with that I run back into the tent, grab my the bag, fill it with food, take up my hair tool in one hand and my staff in the other and start for the mountain.

"You're being stupid!" Disha calls, "You'll die if you go up there, you can't even walk without limping."

"Stop calling me that!" I scream, not even turning to face her. "I'm not gonna die, I'm never going to die. I'm going to defeat death."

"You can't do that! It's impossible," she shouts from behind me.

"Well, if you're so concerned come on and look after me then!" She doesn't respond immediately to this, probably weighing her options and her chances of death. Then I hear her mutter under her breath right before the crunching of leaves and plants offer the telltale sounds that she is following me. We are now on our way to the mountain and what would be held upon it.

XII

She catches up soon without saying a word and we continue in icy silence until we are again at the point of the mountain where it slopes too sharply to walk up. Then, using my torch, I press four holes into the wall and place my feet and hands into them. I continue carving cavities up the height of the mountain, ever holding on with one hand, making a hollow with the other.

Disha follows my example and we're soon making our slow but steady way up the mountain. The stone continues to shake and roar, and at times we're concerned we may be thrown back down the side of the wall, but we cling to the side of the stone structure for our very lives. We're about halfway up, the point where before we had fallen and also a nearly vertical climb when the mountain roars more loudly than it had yet and shakes so violently my feet slip and I clench the mountain with only one hand.

We hear a screaming noise coming from above, and look to where the sky and sun should be we can see only thick, pitch black smoke that creates a tangible darkness. Coming out of the smoke there are lights, bright white and orange, raining down from the sky.

It's fire. Fire is falling from the sky.

I've experimented enough with the strange substance to know that any contact with it will create burns, and unlike the feeling received when one touches the dark stone walls, these burns don't just go away. I clutch the mountain closer as the fire rain falls behind me. I bring up my pace, trying to move more quickly up the mountain, making the glowing handholds shallower than before, anything to get to the top. To succeed in my mission. To defeat death.

As I move closer to the summit, I see the dark smoke is actually death, floating in the air so thickly that it blocks out the light and appears black. I know if I breathe in too much of this death smoke I will surely die. I take the top of my shirt and use it to cover my mouth, keeping as much of the deathly smog away from my breathing as possible. I see Disha follow suit and soon we are engulfed in the black cloud.

I can't see the top of the mountain through the smoke, but I can see that more and more of the fire rain is now falling. Some sort of boiling black ooze is pouring over the rim of the peak and down the walls. I have to quickly move to the left or right a few times as this river of extinction flows down toward me. The mountain shakes, roaring and expelling fire and smoke, it's a violent fight between the two of us and the mountain.

And then, my head is stabbed with pain as potent as before, and my hand slips from the face of the stone.

Falling, I feel myself falling, slipping away from the mountain I'm so determined to climb. So determined to defeat death.

I am going to defeat death.

I make a ridiculous attempt to catch myself and grasp the stone again. I fling my hand forward and prepare to fall.

But I don't. Miraculously, my hand meets with the stone again, though it feels differently, straighter somehow, a sharper corner to grasp. The mountain roars again, as though furious I haven't fallen, and spews forth more fire into the air. I pull up with my hand and see, gloriously, that I have reached the top. I have climbed the mountain.

I can only just see the rough outline of the girl through the dark smoke acting as a wall around me. She is struggling to climb up. "Disha!" I scream over the noise of the roaring mountain, "Grab my hand!"

I don't know if Disha can see or hear me, but I lie down on the edge of the summit and stretch my arm out at her, just brushing her fingers. She looks up and grabs my hand. I pull up with as much strength as I can muster, and have nearly pulled her up when a portion of the oozing black substance changes directions enough to come into contact with Disha's other arm.

Some things are simply too difficult to explain with words. Some things transcend the narrow borders we are able to construct with speech. Language is just too restrictive. The noise that comes out of Disha's mouth at that moment is one such thing. It is more than a scream, more than agony, it is absolute pain and suffering manifested into a single, terrible sound. I know at that very moment that no longer how long I live, whether I beat death or not, that sound will never leave me.

I pull her up to the top of the mountain with me, trying without success to ignore her screams. Once we are standing there, or rather I stand and she crouches in pain, holding her arm, I look around trying to see where to go from here. Looking in the mountain all I can see is smoke and swirling pools of the molten black substance. I looked to the left and right but can see nothing but smoke.

But wait, what's that in the distance? I squint and try to look through the smoke and fire. I can just see a shape, a little darker than the darkness around me. I run over to the shape, leaving Disha for a moment to investigate. I come across a sort of bridge extending over the opening on the top of the mountain. I run over the bridge and see that it ends halfway over the pool of molten death.

At the end of the bridge there's a semicircle opening away from me. Leaning down I see what I hadn't seen for what feels like a lifetime. It's a note. The note is pinned to the stone of the bridge. Leaning down I pluck it from the nail and read its simple and short message.

Jump.

I run back to Disha, not taking even a second to question the word. Reaching her I grab her good arm and try to make her follow me back to the bridge, but she is in too much pain to even realize what I'm doing or likely what's going on at all. I would pick her up but I know there's no way I can actually hold her and move back the thirty or so feet to the end of the bridge. Instead I drag her, holding my hands under her armpits and walking backwards.

She tries to fight me, starts calling out my name and demanding I stop, but I don't and soon we're over the bridge. She must have figured out just what I'm doing because she starts fighting me even harder, twisting her body this way and that. I don't say a word as I finally reach the end of the bridge.

I let go of Disha and crouch in front of her so she can see me. Her face is black from the smoke and soot floating in the air, and I'm sure mine looks similar. "Disha listen to me!" I yell as the mountain shoots a huge plume of smoke and fire into the sky. "I found a note Disha! We have to jump!"

"You're insane!" She screams back, "We'll die. The death will take us and you'll be defeated like everyone else!"

Her words strike my heart, making me question if perhaps she is right. Maybe I will only be burned up and forgotten, another person lost, likely to become just one of the stone people that had terrorized me so much. But I have to do this, I will die if I stay here anyway. I may not be able to defeat death by jumping, but I will greet death on my own terms, and that seems as much victory as I can have right now.

"Maybe you're right," I say, "but I'm gonna try anyway." Disha opens her mouth to protest again, but I grab her again and pull her to the very edge of the bridge. "You make your decision, you can come with me or stay here and die for certain. I'm leaving!"

I take one step backwards, and fall down into the searing heat and buffeting winds of the inner mountain. I flip over and am facing the pool of death as it rushes up closer and closer. Then, in the very center of the pool, right where I am falling, a large bubble forms and pops. The bubble is made of the molten death, and when it pops all of its contents fly at me. I feel it burning my face and body. It is so hot it feels felt cold as it eats me apart. But I continue to fall, gravity pulling me down in my determination. This is my choice.

I fall down, down, down, and then I'm in it. In the death that burns so badly. But, something is wrong. I look around and see that though I am indeed in the black substance I can feel no burning. In fact, the burns that I had felt only seconds ago as a result of the death flying upwards feel now cold and soon fade away entirely. I can't understand it, what's happening? Have I died?

And then I realize that while I have fallen into blackness, it isn't the blackness of the death, it is a hole. I have fallen into a hole that has appeared somehow. Looking around in all directions, including above and below me, I can see nothing but darkness, and I know I have done it. I have escaped the island, I have reached a portal to a new world. And this one, I am determined, will be my home. I will conquer this new world, make it my own, make it run on my rules, my conditions, my judgement. I don't know this world yet, but it will know be by the time I'm done.

I continue falling for a few minutes, and just begin to wonder how long this fall will last when my feet meet with the ground, and as they do, light bursts from beneath them. Looking down I can see grass growing out of the ground that a moment ago had been nothing but emptiness. Mountains rise up and surround the area, trees stretch out towards the sky in a matter of seconds. Behind me a drop turns into a puddle, then a stream, and soon a large river. Hills rise up and curve over the land. Flowers and bushes spread across the grass sporting fruits and bright colors.

I turn all around at the paradise that is spreading out before me. I smile, this is the place I have determined will be conquered and be my new home, and this is the one place I have ever been to that can actually compare to the beauty of my old glade. I laugh into the air, this is winning. I will beat death here.

PART THREE
FALL

XIII

I feel a chill on the back of my neck, and see that the wind is picking up. The trees that materialized seconds ago are waving back and forth in the wind. Many of the bushes are thrashed about from the winds as well. I watch as many leaves and flowers gather in the wind and blow. As I watch I notice something about the mountains.

No matter which direction I turn to the mountains are there, rising into the air. I know what this means with a dread certainty in my heart. The walls are back. They had never really left I know, before they had just been made up by the oceans, but somehow I had wished that through everything I have gone through maybe now I would have been freed from the presence of these stone partitions that keep me from the freedom I so desire, keep me from escaping death.

I don't have to look to the ground to know that it's there, it always is. But I ignore it. This is my home, my world. The death has no power I don't give it, and I don't intend on giving it any. I refuse to even acknowledge its existence, I won't look at it or think about it. Death will not exist here, I won't allow it.

The wind continues to blow and I notice a strange phenomenon beginning to occur. The sun, which a moment ago was just above me, has begun to spin around the sky. It lowers down to the level of the mountain horizon and then spins around and around, causing the shadows to spin in the same way. I grow dizzy and the moving lights hurt my eyes and brain. I cover my eyes and fall to the ground, feeling like I was the one spinning with the winds and sun moving so quickly around me.

It goes on for what feels like forever. I feel sick and curl up on the ground praying it will all stop moving. I lie like this, powerless to make anything stop, when it occurs to me, this is what the world wants. *It* beat me down to the ground telling me I can't change anything here. It showed me paradise and told me it is unattainable and I have just accepted it.

This is not okay. I am the one who beat the island. I beat the mountain. I *will* beat this world. I will beat death. I stand up, look at the spinning sky and leaves moving in the wind around me. I look at all of it, and say simply, "Stop."

Immediately the sun freezes, just above the mountain in front of me. The leaves drop onto the ground, now dead and brown from being ripped off the trees that were their lives. The trees stop blowing in the wind, now stripped of their clothing they are bare and look like hands reaching into oblivion. The sky is much darker and redder now that the sun has moved from its position at the top of the sky to its lower seat. This is where it belongs. Not above me, it isn't better than me. I am the ruler here. I rule. It will not stand higher than I. The world is trying to defeat me by shedding the beauty it had moments ago by stripping the leaves and moving the sun, but I will not be deterred.

I look at the mountains standing on the edge of the land all around me. They stand above me with a form I have not granted. This is not acceptable. They are not in charge here. I am. I raise my right hand out to the mountain on my side and say, "Move." In my mind I conjure a shape it will change to, and before my eyes I watch without surprise as the mountain shifts and melts into a huge archway. I move my arm to each of the mountains and they each shift into shape. Soon the entire area is surrounded by perfectly symmetrical, identical archways that look out on sky.

I examine the river, it flows freely through the hills, which themselves are scattered without order, independently growing throughout. This will not do. I speak and they all melt into one, huge hill that rounds in the center point between the archways, directly beneath my feet. The river moves to flow around the hill like a moat, and bridges summoned directly out of the ground allow paths over the surface of the water in six different places all equidistant from each other.

I stand at the crest of the hill and move all of the trees so that they form woods outside the river circle. Where my bridges over the water stand, there a path runs through the woods, forming a straight line all the way to the archways. I raise up a magnificent seat in the very center of the hill. This throne is one befitting a ruler, one befitting *the* ruler, one befitting me. I sit and let out a laugh.

I look out on my world, the sun behind my head. The kingdom that I have created before me. This world had been formed when I stepped into it, and it has been shaped at my command. I am truly in control here. I look forward where one of the paths runs down through the woods, and there I see an archway in perfect alignment with the path and my chair. Through the arch I can see only darkness, the light from the sun too far away to reach it. I can see from my justifiably elevated seat that there is nothing beyond that archway. No light, no land, no walls. There is nothing beyond the arch.

I smile, there is nothing beyond my rule, I control it all. Yesterday I was controlled by a mountain and some water. Today I move both at my whim. Today I defeat death.

In the time that follows I often take to walking around my domain to examine the contents therein. I observe each tree, all devoid of leaves but standing high in perfect testimony to my power. I find one particular tree directly behind my throne that has the strangest bark running up its trunk. The bark is dark, nearly black, and it doesn't have grooves and channels running along its length in the way most trees do to separate different portions of the wooden armor.

Instead, the tree's bark is solid all the way around and straight up. I search for a while around the trunk, but can find no defect in this tree. Even the branches are perfectly symmetrical to one another, all the same ratio growing from larger to shorter the higher up you look. I like this tree, this tree will be my mark, the testament to my control and perfect order. I place my hand against this tree, to feel its smoothness and hold its shape, knowing what I would emulate in my land and am surprised to feel the slightest hint of heat beneath my palm.

Pulling my hand away, I can see a familiar handprint glowing back at me. This tree, it is somehow made of the stone, the same stone of the mountains and walls. I don't know how this is possible, but I like it too. This will show the world, show the walls and the mountains again that they are not the ones in control, I rule here, and always will. I place my hand more firmly against the tree, imprinting my hand, my mark of ownership on this tree. When people come to see this tree, they will not look first at the stone it was created from, they will see the brand I have placed upon it, and know through this as in everything my power.

I do this sort of thing every now and then, place my mark against something I control, to let anyone know that it is I and I alone who own and rule it. I occasionally summon stone to my throne to write notes and allow them to fly away to who knew where in the wind. I never know who will read these notes, but I want them to have the information I provide.

I write about how I had been forced out of my home in the glade by the cruel whim of fate. How the world had cheated me of the life I had so enjoyed, where I knew how it all worked and how to provide for myself. I write about how I had seen death and had been terrified of it, but how I used that terror to get what I wanted out of life and not be bullied by what the world deemed appropriate. I write about how I had come to the island I had so hated, boxing me in and trying to contain me not with the strict walls of my childhood but with the subtle waves that rolled forever in each direction, mocking me and saying how there was no way I could escape even though the path was visible. I write about how I had overcome the mountain, climbing to the top and meeting it in the face, daring it to tell me I would die. I write about how I had come to a new world, a world within my control, and world that obeys my rule, rather than that of fate's.

I write about how if one wants something in this world, or any world, one simply has to take it. I stared down the world and showed it who was in charge, and so could anybody else. This is how you win in life, this is how you conquer death. You don't give it the option to follow you, you demand it. This is what I have done, and look at me now. I feast on whatever food I care to conjure up from the ground. Design my home to look however I please at the particular time. I even control the sun and mountains.

You may be wondering what became of Disha, I'm sure I can't say. The only thing I can assume is that she proved too much a coward to reach out and grab her fate by the neck and tell it just who was in charge. She probably died up on that mountain, and honestly, if so, she deserved it. If someone can't toughen up and pursue what they want, then they don't deserve to have it. Life isn't about to give anyone freebies or handouts, and the sooner each person can learn that they farther they'll go. And if they can't learn that? Well, then they will die on the tops of the mountains they're too afraid to jump from. This is simply the way the world works.

I do write about Disha sometimes, warning whatever readers I may ever have not to fall into her footsteps. I tell them fortune favors the brave, the bold, those who take their lives for their own and don't just run with it but set its course. I always read these notes before I sign my name, always quite proud at the vast amount of wisdom and sound advice that emanates from them. I'm honestly a bit jealous that I hadn't had such sensible advice when I was alone, wandering through the glade or struggling on the island.

Regardless, I have learned now, and now my prudence will be shared with whatever children have the privilege to read it. This will be my greatest accomplishment I am sure, that my counsel will be the driving force behind so many to follow me, that they will be able to construct a utopia in this criminal world.

I develop my world, making it better and better, never stopping my improvements. I create more of the stone trees, but allow the one behind my head to remain the largest, framing the sun in its branches. I also add designs into the arches, each one depicting a different portion of my life. One of them shows scenes of my birth, another the valley, another the darkness I once entered, the next my home in the glade, then the island, and finally the realm I had created so beautifully.

I also bring flowers and vines into my world, to add to its beauty. It's then that I learn a strange fact. I can create plants such as flowers or bushes, but the plants I create artificially are all made of the same stone structure of the walls and mountains, the same substance as my tree. This means that if I touch any of them they will glow, and I use this ability to infuse them with a light that glows throughout. So what if they aren't real plants? These are stronger. They never die as nothing in my world died. This world is impenetrable.

There is however, one facet of my kingdom I cannot be content with. One particular fact I cannot change no matter how hard I try. The man in the water is missing. I peer into the river that surrounds my throne for hours, trying to see if anything I can do will bring my friend back to me. I try creating fish, thinking that perhaps the motion of the water will bring him back, give him something to play with. But, all of the fish I create are silent, still, stone. They simply sink to the bottom of the river, and do nothing to make the man appear. I try creating an image of him in this water, but this appears to have no effect either. In the end all I ever see when looking into the water is the lightly rippling clear water over a dozen or so feet of sand at the bottom.

I often swim in this water, pretending that I am with the man in the water. I spend large amounts of time just sitting in the sand floating in the sunlight cast over the trees. I enjoy this time, but it does feel empty without a companion. I should say that there are no animals here either, and the leaves covering the ground provide no company in my long days. I have everything I want, and I am happy, but I cannot be happy *with* anyone, for no one exists here with me.

The reason for this is obvious, and does provide me with some level of comfort. No one else is brave enough to come. Disha had died on the mountain because she was afraid to jump, and I'm sure there are more like her, cowering in corners and shadows, afraid to change their lives. I don't know where the man in the water is, but the thought has crossed my mind more than once that he has disappeared because he too was afraid to go though the fire, smoke, and danger of the mountain's interior. This may mean I am left in solitude, but it is the solitude that is earned by reigning as champion over life. It is a mark of heroism and bravery, not an insufficiency of any kind.

And so I continue in my realm, perfecting and enjoying it. Needing no company but my own, for I am the only one worthy of the privileges I have earned. Let anyone challenge my claim, it is easy to see why I am here and they are not.

XIV

I'm just waking from a nap in my throne, which is where I normally sleep and rest, when I notice it. It isn't evident in the leaves that pool along the ground, nor in the archways that stand quietly as portals into oblivion, the silent stone trees grasping at heaven, or the water softly moving in its circuit around my island. What I notice can't be seen in any of these things, but it can be sensed. I sense difference, and it is here.

I arise from my seat and walk through the woods all around my small but rich realm. I can see no physical change in the landscape or outlook of the world, but even still I can't shake the feeling that something here is off, strange, varied. I may not be able to place my finger on the divergence, but I know it exists all the same.

I slowly make my way back to my throne, suspicious and looking over my shoulder. It's only when I have sat down again though that I notice what can only be the source of my perceptions, for there, standing still halfway over the bridge formed directly in front of me, is a man. A stone man, of the same nature I had seen die in the valley and that had started the mountain's eruption on the island. I examine the man standing in front of me without moving. He doesn't so much as twitch or show sign that he is breathing. I know these creatures can make noise, the man in the valley had screamed. I also know that they can sometimes do extraordinary things such as fly. I also know that there were millions, maybe billions of these creatures. I remember with a shudder how they had chased me and grabbed at me when I first came into the glade.

We stay there a few minutes. Me, staring at the man. Him, facing me back. This is the first time I have had the opportunity to really examine one of these men, and I'm for the first time able to see a little more closely what they look like. Though he's a decent ways off, I can still see that he has no facial distinctions such as eyes or a mouth. Where his face should be there's only blank, somewhat round, dark stone. He seems to be wearing clothing, but it's hard to tell because it's the same dark tone as his skin and there isn't a clearly defined beginning or ending to whatever clothing may be there. I continue observing him as he stands frozen in place.

I'm not confident he isn't a threat, but nothing is being achieved by our voiceless rigidity. "Step forward," I say with enough authority in my voice to make it clear just who is in charge in this situation, just who holds the power.

The man continues to stand, holding his position until I speak up again. "Who are you?" I ask, "This is my world. Why are you here?"

The man still doesn't move. I'm beginning to grow annoyed. I am the one in control here, I rule. This person, if you can even call him that, had entered my domain without my blessing or permission, bringing change to my perfect, routine world. I will make him answer for this, and then I will likely punish him for his intrusion.

I rise from my seat and stand directly in front of him. I'm close enough that I'd be able to hear him breathing if he had been, but standing this close confirms that he is apparently existing without breath. He probably doesn't need to eat either, he certainly doesn't have any mouth to eat from that I can see. A plan begins to assemble in my mind, one that I'm crazy about enough to at least try and execute.

"Listen you," I say to the statue of a man, "are there any more of your kind?" The man stands in silence in response. "If there are any more, call them now."

The man turns his head to the left and right, making no sound. Then he turns back to face me and I wonder if he has done anything. Apparently not yet, for after another second he looks directly into the sky and screams a horrendous cry similar to the one the man had made in the valley. I want to cover my ears and cower from the sound that strikes panic into my veins, but I refuse to stand down. I stand straighter and face the sound fully, showing I can handle anything here. I am still in charge.

After a moment or two the man's screaming ceases and he looks down to face me again. Then, from each of the six paths outside of the archways, where there was nothing, six figures approach the hill I stand on. They make their way up the paths, over the bridges, then spread out in front of me. I look at each of the six stone men, a smile forming on one side of my mouth. This is perfect.

"All of you listen to me." It occurs to me here that these men didn't have any kind of name, any way I can refer to them. What are they? They are nobodies, tools I will soon use. They are merely the extra pieces to my puzzle. I think about this and find their title. "Listen to me, Extranos." I see them all stand straighter when I say this, they seemed to approve of the name, not that I care about their approval. "You are here, in my land, under my control. You stumbled in here, some of your own accord, some because you were called, but you will all be used in the same manner.

"You see, I am the ruler here, and what is a ruler without anyone to rule? I am great, mighty, all powerful, but I still need those lower than myself to remember just how far I have come. This is where you, Extranos, come in. You are mindless, stupid even. You do whatever I ask, without any question. I like this, and so I will allow you all to stay here, as my subjects.

"I want you to go through my realm every hour, examining its contents. You will report to me to show me any defects within it. This will allow me to focus my time on expanding my borders and adding to the world in the ways that please me without constantly checking up to make sure everything is still functioning properly. You are not allowed to sleep, not allowed to rest. You will work, or you will leave. You may be wondering what benefit there is for you in my plan. I assure you this world is the one you have looked for, for in this world I will promise you one thing. In my world, there is no death."

This is the first time I've ever seen any kind of emotion from the Extranos. They look to one another and almost seem to vibrate with excitement at my promise. I nearly laugh at their ridiculous show, but maintain myself, keeping still. My promise is of course no lie, but their display on just how easily they may be bought is the naivety of children, which I suppose these creatures must be.

"Well," I say, beginning to wave them off, "get to it then. Leave me to my work, and go get to your own." They all begin to walk off when I am struck with another thought. "Wait! Come back here for just a moment."

The seven Extranos wander quickly back over, some with their heads turned as though confused. "Each of you come and stand before me," I say. The stone men looked to one another and file into a line. I look at the first one standing only a foot or two in front of me. I smile at this man that has given over possession of his life to me, then raise my hand and press it against his face.

As I expect from the stone nature of his skin, my hand leaves a blue glow against his head. I smile and tell the next one in line to step up. In turn I mark each of the men with my handprint, marking for all the world to see that these are my subjects, as much under my control as the archways and the trees here. Even as the sun obeys my orders, so will these mute, dumb, faceless nobodies.

"There," I say upon branding the last one, "now you may go, and don't let me see any of you again until you bring something to me worthy of my time and my attention. Any disturbances I don't deem necessary will result in the excommunication of the subject into the darkness beyond my arches." I turn and sit back down onto my throne. "Now get to work."

And so did the true beginning of my empire occur.

XV

Having the Extranos as my slaves proves a most efficient system. I can sit on my throne throughout the day, making diagrams and designs in my head for the expansion of my kingdom. I extend my borders well beyond the archways, learning that I can materialize the stone to reach out into the oblivion beyond. I create pools of water and gardens full of the foods I had liked best from the glade and the valley. I don't know how, but when I make these gardens the plants that filled them are living, rather than the stone that everything else I make seems to be made of.

There I grow the yellow plants I had with Disha on the island, berries and nuts that I once collected in the glade, and lots of other plants that I had discovered over my life. I have some of the Extranos check the foods I create, to make sure there is no death within them. If any such plant is found in my gardens, it's immediately cast out into oblivion along with all like it. In this way I keep delicious gardens stocked with all kinds of good food and avoid the poisonous plants that might otherwise hand me over to the death.

As the land continues to grow outwards so do I need more attendants to watch over the different districts within my realm. I call more and more of the stone men to my side and appoint them over different regions throughout the land. There each of them is given a specific job, a portion of the land to oversee. They're very efficient at their jobs, and hardly ever bother me to notify me of any problems (so few are the problems to be discovered) so that when I do hear one of their piercing shrieks ring through the air I know it is serious.

So is it that I come running back to my throne from the pools off the southern sector. Coming to my seat I can see a few of the faceless men hopping around the throne looking very anxious and upset over something. I raise both my hands and look at each of them. "What is it? What's wrong with you?"

They all turn, noticing apparently for the first time my presence then look eastward, directly ahead of the chair. I sit down and look down the path, seeing nothing. "Well," I demand, "what of it? What did I tell each of you about bothering me without due cause? Do you think my threats are idle? I will throw each and every one of you out, and then you shall die. We'll start with you-"

Suddenly my words run off as they fall far lower on my list of priorities. For there, maybe two hundred meters in front of me, is a dark shadow. Between the trees, where the light of the sun far behind don't quite reach, there is a person, I'm sure of it. "You there! In the woods! Whoever you are you have managed to enter my land. This is my country, I own it and rule sovereign. You will come and present yourself to me. Come out of those shadows now!"

The shadow takes a few steps forward, then stops just as the light is about to uncover its face. Then it continues after a moment, and I nearly lose all the contents in my stomach. "Extranos," I say quietly to my servants, "leave me. Go and check on the gardens."

The men leave and I sit, looking my visitor in the eye as the distance between us closes. Soon enough she is over the bridge and on the hill. "So," I say almost silently, "you're not dead."

"That's some hello for your only friend," Disha says. "Not even going to ask how I've been? I see you're doing alright." She looks around at my world, seeing the mountains and trees arranged in my order and the Extranos working their sectors. "Quite the place you've got here, discover it all on your own?" I'm still just trying to process how the girl is standing in front of me, for she is a girl no longer. Her face has grown and thinned out, her body taller and leaner. Her hair has completely grown back, leaving no sign of the cut from the island. She walks with grace and poise, seeming to know where every muscle lay and how it functioned. I wonder if I look as differently to her as she does to me. I'm sure I do not, I feel just the same as when I was on the island, save for being more powerful now.

"No," I say, "I created it."

"Ah, I see."

"Why are you saying it like that? Do you not believe me?" I demand, "I can show you. I have forests and gardens, waterfalls and hills. Or I could make a mountain, or even move the sun, I have infinite power here."

"No doubt you think you do," she says.

"It is apparent that your loose lips have not lost their edge," I say testily. "I made everything you see here, by my hand and imagination was it built. Don't you see? This is Utopia."

"Well, I'm afraid I highly doubt that," she says, "it doesn't look all that great to me, and how do you know you created it?"

I'm struck with confusion, "What do you mean? Don't you think I would know if I created something? Watch this!" And with that I extend my arm to the space between both of us and up from the rounded earth of the hill shoots a tree, dark and stiff. It rises higher and higher growing braces that extend over both of us. "Can't you see? I created this tree, I can create anything."

"I don't see any tree," Disha says quietly. She takes a few steps around the tree so she's on my side, then to touches the trunk with her hand. A familiar reddish glow appears on the surface. "This is a rock. Trees are alive, they drink water and breathe in sunlight. This is just a cold, dead statue."

Suddenly I'm standing to my feet, furious. "You will refrain from using that word here! Nothing is dead here, there is no death, I have defeated it. It doesn't exist."

Disha looks confused by my statement. The stupid girl can't even understand what I'm talking about. But in her eyes there's another emotion, deeper than confusion, it almost looks like, like… pity.

"You can't really defeat death Peri," Disha says, staring at me in the eye with that stupid look. "I hoped you'd grown out of that obsession. Death is inevitable, but you don't need to fear it. Death, death is apart of life."

"You're insane," I say, "death is the opposite, the end of life. Of course you can defeat death, just because no one has doesn't mean no one can. I will be the first, the only perhaps, but I will accomplish this. I've already cast it out of my land."

"Why are you so afraid?" she asks, "And why do you think you've gotten rid of death here? You think your towers and gardens are keeping you safe?" Disha leans down and digs something out of the ground.

"What are you doing?" I demand, "Stop that digging!"

She stands back up and holds something in her hand, I refuse to look. "Peri, what's in my hand?"

"I don't know, and I don't care."

"It's death Peri."

"No, no it's not, there is no death here. I have eliminated it, I have beaten it."

"Just because you deny something or try to hide from it doesn't mean it doesn't exist! It's right here but you're trying to act blind to it. Why? Because you're afraid it will hurt you, you're afraid you're not as powerful as you believe."

I whirl on her, "You impudent child! How dare you say that to me?"

"Because someone has to tell you!" Disha yells back, "Look around you Peri, wake up! Everything is dead here. Notice there are no animals here? It's because there's no life. There aren't even leaves on the trees, they all fell off because you can't sustain them. You think you run everything but honestly you run nothing. And why? Because right outside that arch and a little ways down a path there is nothing, there is the oblivion that is waiting to swallow everything you think you've built up here in your dead stone kingdom. Honestly, do you even see what these trees are made of? These are the walls Peri, the walls you once hated so much, the walls you wanted to get past. Now you've just built them up yourself! You think you escaped death when in reality all you're doing is offering it a comfortable place in your world."

"Don't believe me?" she continues, "Just try to leave this place, if you're all powerful you should be able to destroy it all and start anew, make any world you want. Only this time, make it without stone walls and an earth of death. Try all you want though, you won't be able to do it. Because while you're putting on a blindfold and saying you've got control death is closing in and laughing at your ignorance and naiveté in thinking you ever had anything at all."

"Enough!" I roar, "Extranos come now! Take this stupid girl and throw her out of the borders into the oblivion." I walk closer to Disha while the stone men appear and hold her on either side. I stare her in the eye, anger blazing within me. "You see this? You see these slaves that follow me? We once ran from these creatures, but I own them now. And now your time has been used up. I tire of your company, you'll now be executed because you're nothing more than a used toy to me."

"You may want to reconsider that proposal," a voice says from nowhere. My eyes widened as I look at Disha, whose mouth hasn't moved.

I materialize a knife out of the air and hold it at Disha's throat, a purple glow rising on the heating blade between my hand and her neck. "What is that voice?" I scream. She stands there, pinned by the Extranos and held by my knife, looking me in the eye but refusing to say anything. "Tell me Disha! Or we'll see if you're right about there being death in this world!"

The girl smiles beneath my knife, "What's wrong Peri? Don't like not being in control?"

My eyes flare and I press my knife harder, causing the girl to shriek out as a small cut is made. The knife is beginning to grow unbearably hot but I refuse to give up before the girl. We stand there, the blade glowing blindingly bright. I can see tears appearing in the girl's determined eyes, but still she refuses to back down. My hand feels as though it has seared with the knife, as though I've reached the point where it can no longer be removed when the voice calls out again.

"You know you're not really proving anything to anyone with this display? It's rather disappointing honestly, particularly for the ruler of the world and all."

I spin around, evaporating the knife in my hand with silent relief. I looked around for the source of the voice but can see nothing.

"Oh don't tell me that you can't find me, really I expected more from one such as yourself."

I run towards the voice, it seems directly in front of me, but at the same time it's like it's coming from all around me. I run down the hill a little.

"There we go, you're getting warmer now, though I don't suppose that's what you want to hear after getting rid of that knife is it? No, that's why you got rid of it. Just couldn't handle the pain, that burning suffering calling into the center of your soul, beyond all control and tolerance. Oh, and I guess the physical pain was pretty bad too huh?"

My cheeks begin heating up, it feels like my ears are on fire. I continue following the voice until I'm standing on my bridge, looking all around. "Where are you?" I call out, "Stop taunting me and show yourself you coward!"

"Coward," the voice says, "what an interesting title granted by one who won't even look at death for fear it may exist beyond one's control. Yes, that's very interesting indeed. I do believe you could see me, if you only remembered what it is to be humble and look down."

What is this demon on about? Humbling myself and looking down? Looking down, down to what? I realize instantly where I am standing as my blood freezes in my veins and all heat vanishes. I am on the bridge, which is over...

Looking below me, and just off the bridge, I see a man.

A man in the water.

XVI

The man is in the water, and yet he's not apart of the water as he always was in the past. Instead, the man stands upright to his knee in water just under the bridge looking up at me. Even for this difference in perspective though, I can see immediately this is the same man of all my memories. Though he now looks older in the same way Disha does, it is clear he is the one person who has stayed with me throughout my life.

No, he hasn't stayed with me, he abandoned me before the mountain erupted. He hadn't come to my land until now. Things are different now, after all I have done, after his long desertion. "It's you…" I stutter, "You, you're out of the water."

"Well," the man says, looking down at his legs, "I wouldn't quite say I'm out of the water yet as it were." He raises a leg and watches the water drip off of it. "No, I'm fairly certain I am still in water."

My mouth drops at this unexpectedly facetious response, so uncharacteristic of the man I had once known. Of course, he had never spoken independently before, so how well do I really know him? "No but you're… you know, not in the water. Like you used to be, you got out."

"Ah well yes," the man says, "I suppose you're right enough there. Though to be fair I was always able to leave the water, I just never needed to before. You always looked for me in the water, you wanted to know me and how I felt about things. In recent days, you haven't been quite so, how shall I say it? Receptive?"

I am confused, I'm angry, I'm hurt. "What are you talking about?" I scream at the man as I jump down into the water and look at him at eye level. "Do you know how long I searched for you? All the ways I tried to bring you back! I was scared when you left me, I was alone! You're the one who denied me, disappearing without a trace!"

"You didn't want me. You wanted the friend who agreed with you and played games with you. That was never who I was. I am more than a playmate Peri."

"What are you talking about?" I demand.

"Think about when I left you, Peri. Was I the one who changed? Were you the same child you were in the glade? Do you think nothing in you has changed?"

"Of course nothing changed! I'm still me, I've always been me, this entire time, my whole life!" The man in front of me looks at me, not saying a word, just drilling me with his eyes. Those eyes hold a blend of emotions, something between pity and... is it amusement? "Do you find something funny?"

"You're so different from who you once were. Once all you wanted was to be able to play and help your friends. You wanted to live in peace and you allowed the world around you to move in whatever way it chose, you just wanted your friends to be safe. You were curious, inquisitive about the world around you. You then only ever wanted to learn, not dominate. You didn't want to create, you wanted to understand. Those were the days when you had friends instead of subjects. You changed, it happened on the island, but it started even before that, even in the glade you had begun to fall into the darkness you now consider your proper home. Look around you Peri, there is no life here, no happiness-"

"I was a child in that glade!" I shout, cutting the man off. "If I've changed it's because I grew. You, and you too," I say pointing back at Disha, who still stands by my throne, "You both want me to give up everything I have created. You say that I have done these terrible things, but I am a good person! Neither of you have ever had the ambition I embraced, never thought to see some potential beyond the world around you."

"There is no potential here Peri," Disha says, breaking free of the Extranos and coming over to us, "You haven't actually accomplished anything, nothing of any real significance. Your so-called power still can't give you the life you so desire by humoring your incessant, self-inflicted hunger for more. You miss the opportunities you have now because whenever you achieve something you just look for what you can conquer next."

"You will never be able to defeat death," the man says, "and you're going to lose the chance to succeed in life if you won't even look at it for more than a second."

"I do look at my life," I says, "more than either of you. I'm not blinded by complacency, I don't just accept what life throws at me without a fight."

"That's all you ever do is fight," Disha says.

"Only because the world is determined to battle with me!" I roar. "Only because no matter how settled into a place I get, no matter how long I know someone, no matter how much good I do my home will be taken away, my friends will leave me, and in the end I will still die. I'm fighting because the system is unjust, can't you see that? It's broken, and it should be fixed."

"And you can change it?" the man says, "You have some real kind of power that will make this death covering everything disappear, bother no one anymore, including yourself? If you have this power, I'd like to see it."

I'm growing angrier and angrier, but also I just feel sad. These two were my friends, the only two I had ever really had. I had known lots of animals in the glade, but they were not capable of the relationships I'd had with these two people, or at least that I'd thought I'd had. I am sad because these two that I honestly do care about so deeply simply can't see the obvious flaws in their view of the world. They honestly think you can get through life in a world that wants to cheat you of everything you deserve and work for. They are naive, but I can't seem to make them see reason.

I take a breath, trying to calm down, then I slowly walk away from the two of them to my throne. I turn to one of the stone men standing there and tell them to go collect some food from my gardens. I sit in the chair I had grown from the ground and fold my hands, then lean my head against them. I'm just beginning to feel a headache coming on. "Look you two," I say after a moment, "why don't we all settle down? You both can stay here if you like, for as long as you want. If you want to leave, that's fine too."

A silence falls on the hill. The Extranos return with a few platters of assorted fruits. "Eat, you should recognize all of it," I say tossing one of the yellow fruits to Disha. She catches it and they both look down on it, as though considering whether they will accept my food. Like it's some kind of compromise. Eventually they both come closer and begin eating. I raise up seats for the both of them and we all take an icily silent meal.

When we have finished eating I stand in the awkward circle, "I don't know about both of you, but I'm tired, it's been a trying day. If you want anything, just ask one of the Extranos, they'll get it for you. Goodbye." Then I walk into the Northern Sixth's woods, through the archway, and continue walking until I am far enough from the sun to keep all light out. Still I continue walking, trying to get away from the conflicting emotions and inward argument raging in my head.

Who were these two to come back in my life after abandoning me to tell me I'm the one who is wrong? I want them with me, I want things to be as they had been, but now we can all have the power to actually control our lives. I want to bring life, what was so bad about all of that? Why do they attack me for wanting nothing more than to be free of the constraints the world always tried to place on me? Can they really claim to want anything different in their own lives? Am I really any kind of problem?

I continue walking, beyond the trees, beyond the grass, until eventually I meet it, the end. I look out at the oblivion that stretches out beyond the cliff that is the edge of my world. I can only just see the faint outline of land in this blackness beyond the sun. Looking directly forward I can see only thick, tangible darkness.

I know I can create more land into this darkness if I want to, and for some reason I feel like proving this to myself. I begin creating an outstretch of land that stretches forward, only a few feet across, into the border of night. I begin walking out, and then start running into the night, confident that the ground will appear below me as I move onwards. I run out into the night farther and farther. The darkness feels almost stifling but still I continue to run.

And then, just as I feel it had gotten so dark there can't possibly be anything beyond, I see lights. There are lights in the darkness all around me. Tiny pinpricks of white break through the sheet of blackness surrounding me on all sides. At first there are only a few of the lights scattered, but then as I watch more and more surface, shining into the darkness. Soon there are hundreds of thousands of the lights casting a glow over me.

I reach my hand out to catch one of the lights, but they are apparently farther away than I thought. I take a few steps into the darkness, materializing the ground beneath me as before, trying to get to the lights, but it seems that no matter how near I get they are always further. Finally I have to accept that these lights are simply too far away to grasp and I sit down on the edge of my stretch of land.

I sit there, hovering over oblivion, considering everything my life has led to. I look out at these lights, "Stars" my mind calls them, and wonder at them. They are so beautiful, capturing light in a subtle, glorious manner. I have never seen anything like them before. I love them.

I wonder if I fall from this cliff right now if I will just continue falling into the stars forever. I would be able to escape the problems determined to chase me down, maybe even create a world where I can just drift among the stars forever. I can just give up on trying to defeat death and instead accept my fate among the thing I find most beautiful, these stars.

I stand to my feet, step up to the very edge of the cliff face, and look out over the stars. All it would take is one step more, then a new life will be mine, or maybe it would be the end of a life. It may be fast, without much pain, I guess that wouldn't be too bad. Would I actually even die if I just kept falling? There is no death here, floating in the air, so I don't see how I could, but I can't really be certain until I take that step and begin my fall.

I'm ready to do it, ready to fall into the beauty of the stars and accept whatever consequences present themselves. I'm ready, but then I remember again Disha and the man. I had been so certain they would be happy in my world, enjoy the life I had created for myself, but they despise it, they believe it to be evil somehow. What if I am wrong and they're the right ones? If I just disappear what will happen to them? What will the Extranos do? Would they wander around my world forever, keeping to their appointed tasks, or would they go wild, running through caves trying to capture innocent people as they had once with me?

I don't know what will happen if I leave now, not only to myself, but also to everyone else. Do I care though? They have all managed without me before, they can surely do it again. I can have what I want and they can go back to the lives they led before.

But then, the main reason the man and Disha think I'm doing something wrong is because they think it's selfish. If I did do this, it would be only because I want it, I don't even know what they would think of it.

XVII

I don't know exactly what it is that motivates me to walk away from that ledge, but it went back to those two and what they would think of it. I'm not a good enough person to say that it's because I want them to be happy or give them what they want. No, I want to prove to those two that I am not selfish. I want to prove that everything I have done is for more than vanity or ignorant pride. I will show them just how wrong they have been about me and about everything. And then, when they apologize for accusing me falsely, we can live in my world happily. Then we will have no problems between the three of us, everything will be back to normal, we can all be friends.

I turn my back on the world of stars I have come to, and walk the long way back to the cliff on the border of the world. I continue walking until I'm about halfway through the woods. It's still fairly dark here, so I make up a bed, and go to sleep. My dreams are filled with visions of the stars, me sailing through them, being truly free in a way I have never experienced. There are no problems, no disagreements among the stars, just peaceful flying through the lights. I would stay there forever if I didn't wake up.

When I do arise from the bed, I walk back to my throne on my central hill, which is unoccupied at present. I take my seat and call for one of the stone men to get me some food. I eat in the silence that falls from my solitude, but am interrupted when I hear the piercing cry that means one of the Extranos has found something. After the events of yesterday, I nearly don't go, but I have to.

I began running into the west where I had heard the beacon of sound. I found the source just a little ways into the woods. An Extrano is looking at one of the stone trees. "What is it? What's the problem?" I ask seeing nothing out of the ordinary. The Extrano raises one hand and points to the side of the tree opposite me. I walk over and my mouth drops in shock.

The tree…is rotting.

In the stone that makes up the trunk of the trees I created there is a hole, as though it's been bitten out of and ripped apart. I gingerly touch the rough edges, causing them to lightly glow. "What could have done something like this?" I ask, but of course the stone man makes no reply. I bring up more stone from the earth and mend the rip in the tree, smoothing it out as best I can and try to make it look as though nothing is wrong.

I'm almost finished when I hear another scream, deeper in the forest off to my left. I run to the sound, afraid of what I'll find and feel my blood turn to ice as I see another Extrano standing by a tree pointing at a developing bite out of the stone trunk. I look on it and then hear another cry, and then another, and another. All throughout my world my servants are screaming out their warnings, the alerts ringing out everywhere, bringing to light just what is happening. My world, my perfect world without eat or decay or sadness, is dying.

I fall to the ground, slumped there in the middle of the woods while the Extranos' cries continue to ring out all around me. I feel like I am falling, drowning in the emptiness that is the silent destruction of everything I have created. It is like the world is yet again mocking me, ironically making me feel as though I am falling in pain after my dream of flying through starlight.

"And so it begins, the end of all things," a now familiar voice says behind me. I don't turn to look at the man from the water. I know what he will try and tell me. He will mock me along with the rest of the world, shame me for wanting to rise to anything at all. He will try to crush me into the dirt and death. They, all of them, the man, Disha, the rest of the world are all laughing at me, striving to make me powerless.

I know then, I know I was right in not jumping into the stars before. No, I had to come here, I will show every one of them that I am not just a leaf in the wind blown this way and that, I am the tree that can stand tall and take the beating. I whirl around to the man and glare at him.

"You did this! You're destroying my world out of spite!" I roar at him.

"I did nothing more than watch as your actions were carried out," he says, "I told you you could not keep death out, that you were just destroying life creating this paper kingdom, but you wouldn't listen to me. This is the result." He gestures all around us at the cacophony of noise rising higher and higher as more Extranos began screaming.

"This is not my doing!" I shout over the din of voices. "Nothing was wrong until you and the girl entered my land, and now look at it, look at what you have started!"

"Continue blaming us if you wish," the man says calmly, "It will change nothing, the death of this world will still inevitably fall. You cannot save it so long as you don't change."

"You want change?" I demand, "You want it to be saved? Fine, I will clean up the mess you have brought on." I close my eyes and focus on this world, on every detail that I had so carefully added from the smallest berries and branches, to the mountains and sun itself. I consider everything I have made and think about how it is now dying. It needs some renovation is all, like I patched up the tree before, that's all that needs to happen. I stretch out both my arms apart, spread my hands out fully. Then in one deliberate, huge thought begin changing everything, healing the entire world around me.

I let out a scream as trees mend their cloven trunks, plants regrow and ripen, rocks stand back up where they have crumbled. I let out a roar and feel a physical pain with all of the power crashing through my mind and body and out into the land all around. My cries join those of the stone men everywhere, creating a hurricane of noise. I can feel the mending process begin, and soon feel the wounds on my creations close up as though they are cuts on my own body.

I open my eyes to look at the tree in front of me. I can just see the last bits of bark closing in, recreating the tree's perfection it previously possessed. I sigh and lower my arms as all is healed again. After a minute or two the Extranos stop screaming, having noticed that the problems have been mended.

I smile and look at the man, "Convinced yet? Now do you understand that I do indeed have the power to keep death from this, and any world I choose?"

The man looks at the tree, sees where it had been mended, but he only looks sad. "Unfortunately," he says, still looking at the tree, "I'm afraid I'm not."

Then from far off, the stone men begin to scream into the air again, their symphony of cries ringing out anew. I look to the tree beside me and see the hole reopening, as though the layer of stone I placed on it is melting. "No!" I growl and stretch my hand to the tree, bringing more and more stone to it. I will place the rock in the right place, line it up where it belongs, but it seems even as I mold it into place it begins again melting down. I run to the tree and crouch beside it. I push the stone with my hands, physically holding it in place to keep it from melting off, ignoring the heat that burns against my skin, but it just falls over my hands, sinking back into the earth below me.

I try everything I can to keep the tree alive, but the hole only continues to grow, running the whole length of the trunk and spreading into the branches. Soon what had once been a proud sentinel over my domain becomes nothing more than a thin stalk of stone barely held above the ground. Then, even this sinks down, finally bubbling in a puddle on the surface, before even that disappears before me. I sit there, bent before my creation that is now nothing. I sit there as nothing myself but a failed attempt at success.

"This doesn't have to be an end, Peri," the man says behind me, "You can still change, come with me, remember who you used to be. We can fix this."

I am too tired, too distraught to argue with this fool from the water. I manage to mutter out the words, "Leave me," before I fall against the ground, feeling like I too am melting into the earth, leaving it all behind.

I hear nothing for a few seconds, and then the man's footsteps begin falling, growing quieter and quieter as they move away from me. And there I lie, nothing more than an insignificant ruler of a world melting to ruin. It has taken many days and much effort to create and build up, and now, in the space of a few hours, it is all gone. Leaving once and for all until there is nothing left but a broken figure lying on its surface.

And the death, lots of the death.

Peri

I lay there, longer than I can account, feeling as though I am melting more and more into the ground. The death and I are now one. After all my fighting it, all my determination to finally defeat death, I have passed into it voluntarily. It is just another punchline on the continuing joke that is my life.

The ground continues to fall down and level out. The stone men melt back into the ground with the trees and mountains. The rivers and ponds fade from existence, either disappearing into the sky or sinking far into the ground. Even the hills flatten and leave the entire world one long, seemingly endless tablet stretching outwards. The sun falls below the horizon and everything goes black.

And then, it begins to rain.

The water falls from the sky to quietly plunk into the death creating a layer of moisture over everything, as though trying to clean away the idea that my kingdom had ever existed, my "paper kingdom" as the man from the water had said. If that is the water's aim, it is doing it well, no one could ever know by looking at this desolation that it had once been anything else.

Still I lay there, somehow conscious while also most certainly being dead. This must be what happens when the death takes you. You simply wait forever as the world becomes increasingly meaningless and the rain falls to wash your existence away. Maybe this actually happens your whole life, you just didn't realize it until you die. If this is all my life amounted to, had it ever meant anything? I couldn't accomplish my primary goal, to defeat death, so really what had I ever managed to do?

Nothing. I accomplished nothing. I was nothing.

And now, I am simply less of nothing.

I continue in this way forever. Ages and eternities pass like they do in life, but now I can see them go. The world eventually moves again, but I don't bother to take note, it is meaningless anyway. I am dead, who cares what happens to the world or how it changes? Nothing can truly be accomplished with it or through it. I close my eyes, and let it all pass on.

PART FOUR
WINTER

XVIII

I hear the groaning of the world, stretching this way, trying on different outlooks and seeing how it can stand. I suppose eventually it must find its preferred scape, for it stops moaning and swaying this way and that, leaving me to my peaceful inexistence. I'd have been content to remain dead in my defeat for the rest of eternity, but I am disturbed by something cold falling onto my nose. Opening my eyes, I see a wonder.

The stars are everywhere, just as I once dreamed. Not only are they far off in this pitch black sky, but they are dancing all around me in the wind as well. There are stars far away and stars falling onto my face. There are so many stars on the ground that I can step into them and leave footprints. These stars are magical, and I am sure that this is what it feels like to fly, to exist among the heavens where the stars play around you.

I run through the stars, feeling many of them brush me and stick to my clothes, they are so cold! I hardly notice though, I am in such awe of where I am.

As the stars dance around me and I dance through them, I become disoriented and eventually get lost. Looking around, all I can see is the white surrounding as thousands and thousands of stars pile onto the ground and the blackness is interrupted by occasional stars into the skies. I can't tell one area from another, and the only indication that I had ever even been here at all is found in the trail I leave in the cold substance on the ground.

That's it, the only trace at all. I suppose I must not be dead after all, I suppose I have to go on living. I think about my world I had left. Had it ever truly existed? Maybe it had all been a dream conjured up by my feeble mind yearning to find the one place where death was no more and I could truly be free. Maybe the man in the water and Disha had been right, perhaps it had all been the selfish result of one person's close minded ambition.

Peri

Even as I think it I can feel my cheeks becoming hot and my temper start to flare up a little. Of course *I* wasn't the problem, that's ridiculous, I've told myself as much a million times before. The problem with my world had lain in its most inherent flaw: that other creatures existed within it. I laugh into the air as I have this revelation. The problem hadn't been me, it had never been me. No, the problem was simply that there was anything more than me.

It was probably the Extranos, those stone men cause destruction wherever they step, and in the end they brought it to my world. Yes, this all makes sense. My world had been perfect, but when you give gruntlings perfection what can you expect but for them to mar it?

I'm smiling to myself at this proposition, quite pleased with this scenario when the wind suddenly picks up and in an instant is of cyclonic force physically spinning right where I stand over the slippery, cold stars.

What am I saying? Have I learned nothing? Of course the problem hadn't been the Extranos, they always did their jobs with full efficiency and productivity. They were one of the few things I could trust in this world. They're wild enough yes, but with my training they had been able to keep my entire domain in check, allowing me to focus on larger affairs. No, of course the problem hadn't been with my servants, it had to have been with their master.

Who can be faulted more if a country goes into ruin than her leader? I am the one who raised up the world, and somehow I must have done so badly. There must have been some sliver or crack in the ground that I missed, some agent of death slipping into my trees. Obviously something I created had gone horribly, horribly wrong. I can never blame the stone men, they don't deserve that after they had so long served my land well and helped it thrive to the level it had achieved. The sun rose on that world, and it set on me.

And so is the sun gone now, and though the stars do provide a beautifully soft light over everything, it's difficult to see more than a few feet in front of me. I remember how brightly the world seemed as a child, how I once had always been able to see the hope in my life, has that changed? I begin walking as I consider the possibility and am surprised when I feel my feet come across not the stars collecting on the ground but a hard rock surface. I look down and see that I've happened across a stone floor of sorts. I look up and see, to my amazement, that this floor slopes upwards higher and higher.

Due to the stars floating in the air I can't see the shape the stone makes in front of me, but I can just make out a dark outline going up and taking most of the view. I look up, trying to find where this outline ends, where its top rests, but can see nothing. I look until my neck feels as though it is bent nearly all the way back, and I see the faintest glow of a light. It's so small I may have mistaken it for a star, but this light is different somehow. It's yellower than the typical white color of the stars, and it has a softer glow. I know somehow that this is the top of this structure.

It has to be some kind of mountain, that's the only possibility that makes any sense. I have never seen anything else that comes close to the massive scale of this colossus sitting in stars. The realization makes me uncomfortable, remembering the mountain on the island and how unstable it had been, even exploding into a fiery chaos of death. I have no guarantee that this mountain will not do the same, I don't think I could make it through such an experience twice.

I step off the mountain's step and consider my options. I can take my chances and climb this mountain, going wherever it leads me and likely facing death, or I can walk among the stars. It's entirely possible that there are other mountains or landmarks hidden beyond the stars here, I can search for them and try to find something safer than this risky endeavor. I can easily look, but deep inside, deeper than I fully understand, I know that such a pursuit would be in vain. There is nothing else in this world, and just because I want a safe existence dancing in stars, I know that sometimes one has to be responsible and take the risks that may kill you, because otherwise you'll never live, never grow. I had tried being selfish and sitting back away from harm, and it hadn't saved me anything.

I walk back to the stone bed and take a step up. I feel as though the entire mountain shudders, but maybe that's just my body in its nervous panic. I have no knowledge of what's to be found on this mountain, and my life has had no shortage of horrors. Despite this justified fear I take another step, and another. I make my way, plodding along slowly, looking around as I do. After walking a bit, I notice the dark outline seems to have moved all around me. I walk over to my right and soon see something that chills my blood to the temperature of the stars.

Here, on this mountain, there are walls.

It takes only a second to recognize the fuzzy image of a wall in front of me, it's of the same variety as the kind I had grown up within. I look all around me, trace the walls with my eyes, and I soon come to the startling realization that I recognize this place. I have been here before, but when? I rack my brain searching for the answer, till suddenly it comes to me. This was where I started. I remember back at the beginning of my life when I had been trapped in the cave with the death coating the floor. Remembering how even then my life had been on the line reminds me of the terror I hold the death with. I managed to leave that place though, getting nearer to death than I'd ever been before, and I came into that room with the door.

That is where I am now, I can see no door here, but the walls and floor are exactly the same, though the death doesn't make up the ground here. What can this mean? How had I ended up back here, and why is this place on this mountain in the stars? There are simply too many question, and I feel as though I am a child again, not understanding anything around me or knowing how to survive. I smile a bit as I remember with a certain nostalgia the innocence I once possessed. I had been so ignorant of the world around me.

I suppose I must have blinked even as I think this, for I open my eyes, and the world changes. I'm still on the mountain, the walls are still on my sides, the stars still fly thorough the air in their random and beautiful patterns, but aside from these things nothing seems the same.

For one thing there's grass sprouting up around my feet and even a few trees. I can see a river running down the path, only this one looks more like a stream than the full size river it seems to move as. It takes me a moment to realize that I am in the valley I had been born into. I recognize the woods that I had looped through so many times in looking for an exit, the river is where I had first met the man in the water, where we tried to get him out of the liquid so we could learn about the world together. I recognize the way the walls sit just so, opening widely into the circular canyon I spent years in.

Things were so very different in that short time. A time that to me seemed to drag on forever. I had been so quick to trust whatever things I found, be they plants, or foods, or objects. I had been an entirely different person in that first stage of my life. A person that didn't understand what it was to be selfish, one who only wanted to experience good things and have fun. Learning had been so fun, discovering the wonders my world held and displayed so prominently around me.

I remained that way in that world, and maybe I would have continued in that lifestyle till now, but that world, the world that had seemed so hopeful and fun, the world that tricked me into thinking it was safe and engaging, that world betrayed me. The first time my trust had been shattered by that seemingly peaceful time had been the stone man, the first Extrano I had ever seen. I thought he would be my friend, I thought he could help me learn about this world. I had only been there for moments but he had experienced more time, surely he had been going to help me. That's what I had been so sure of.

I suppose he had helped me in a way, it hadn't been his fault when death took him, he couldn't help it. And yet, the death *had* taken him, he had died right before my then innocent eyes. His screams of absolute terror had so captured me, freezing me to the spot as I watched him disappear below the surface.I hadn't been able to do anything to save the man, and he hadn't any way to save me. I had learned that day that death was to be feared, that pain existed, and it was scary.

But the world hadn't settled itself there, it was not content to frighten a child and leave him be. No, the world had more in store for me. I had been so ignorant of death and its deceitful ways of hiding in seemingly innocent forms. Sometimes it looked like the moss I had been taught to fear, and other times it disguised itself as foods like the mushrooms I had eaten.

I can clearly see the miniature clearing on the ground where I had taken the vile fungus. My stomach still clenches as it remembers the meal containing death. I try not to think of the sickness it had brought on too long. Soon after the mushrooms I had learned just how I was to get out of the woods in the valley, by writing the note on the wall. I look at the wall on my left and saw, glowing blue against the dark surface, the very note I had written as though I had only just lifted my finger.

The note reads about the man in the water and the mushrooms and the man in the water. I chuckle as I see the crude drawing of the mushroom, I had had a bit of practice since that early time, that time that feels an eternity ago. I look over all of these signs from my childhood, seeing again the person I once was. It's true that the world cheated me in that time, but I hadn't known enough to think of it that way at the time. I had thought that all I experienced was simply normal, I didn't know enough to know I deserved better.

I take a few steps forward on the mountain, and again must have blinked for everything immediately disappears and I am back on the cold mountain in the stars. I looked around at the walls, wondering how they can be so high and yet allow me to see the stars beyond them and allow the stars to fly through them. It hurts my head to think about it too much so I soon give up trying and merely accept that some things happen without me understanding them. Maybe I hadn't always possessed the ability to do this, just accept that some things happened because they were supposed to, but seeing the places where I once lived, remembering the person I once was, I find it in me to feel that way again, for this one moment at least.

As I walk on I soon come to a sudden wall directly in front of me. Looking up I see that it isn't a real wall, but rather a cliff coming off a path above me maybe six or seven feet up. It looks difficult to climb but I still jump and grab hold of the edge. After struggling a bit I pull up enough to get an elbow and then a leg above the short cliff and is soon standing on the new path.

I am only a little surprised to see here another seeming miniature model of a world I had once been too, but this one is far more special to me. Looking around I see the few ponds dotting the land, the winding path cut sharp by the walls, the forests full of good foods and plenty of animals. The ponds seem to have actual fish swimming around, minding their own business as they were ever known to do.

Peri

I lean in on one of the forests, and can see the trails lightly marked into the ground by multiple trips made on short legs. I see the squirrels and rabbits that had been my friends as a child, the ones I shared afternoons with, exploring all the glade in search of adventure.

I had been able to dream then, create whole worlds within my mind, worlds that were happy and safe, worlds that death really couldn't touch. It seems my best leadership had been over my visionary lands, rather than my physical ones. I remember spending hours on my pond island imagining what it would be like to fly like birds, or hold my breath as long as fish. The only limits to my creative power then had been basic hunger or tiredness, when I could no longer maintain the dream.

Food had always been available in that time, and there was always plenty to share with my friends. I had friends then, lots of them. The first stage of my life may have seemed like it lasted forever, but this portion had gone too fast. Maybe that's what motivated me so strongly to fight death, to conduct the hours and hours of research on the strange substance to try to figure out how it could be destroyed, always unsuccessfully of course, but it didn't matter then. The goal was more about the journey than the destination then. I was young, I had time to live, I didn't fear death as an imminent threat but rather as a distant suggestion that only very occasionally came close.

I look all around me at the walls. I had tried not to see them, tried not to remember too vividly a world I could no longer return to, a world that had been snatched away from me with the rude awakening that I was not a child anymore. But still they glare out, the blue light swirling around me in the stars, causing a sea of light dancing in circles in this makeshift glade. Looking at them now I can see the hundreds, perhaps thousands of drawings I had etched there. I can see the notes I had taken on the death and the glade in general. Sharing what foods were good together and where you could find certain sorts of stones. I documented the location of all my favorite nooks to hide in the woods. I smile as I read some of these notes, amazed at just how many of these places I have completely forgotten about. Indeed I remember far fewer than I had

Peri

forgotten. Some of the pictures were of the man in the water, which makes me a bit sad.

I remember how I would sometimes do nothing but sit and talk to the man in the water, telling him how I thought the world worked, hearing him say the same thing at the same moment. We two were always in sync back then, but somehow we wandered away from the place we had once occupied. No, I have no idea where the man has gone, I know not if he was dead or lost forever, maybe he's running his own world now, or maybe he found someone else to talk to from his seat in the waves. He isn't with me though, and that much is probably my fault. He was right, I had been selfish, and now I am alone.

"It's good to hear you say so," a voice says. Looking into the river I can see the source was the man, now in the water as I had always remembered him. I bend down, sitting on my knees beside the water's edge and look sadly at the man in the water. He looks sad, but in an almost embarrassed way. "You know," he says, "I never meant to hurt you by warning you. I honestly want the best for you, it wasn't me acting in jealousy or anything. The same is true of Disha, we really only wanted the best for you."

I don't say anything in response to the man, I just sit looking at some of the drawings on the walls here, drawings I made in another life. "You remember all the things you did there?" the man says from below me. "It was a time when you were content to let the hours pass and pursue hopeless causes and worthless research. You could spend hours dreaming or talking then. Your biggest concerns were never for you but for your friends, always wondering if the death and taken them or if they had enough food. You changed from that person Peri, it was that person I wanted you to come back to."

"Maybe you're right," I say still looking at the wall, at the drawings, "I did want different things then. But then, I was a child, how can I know I wanted the right things then? What if I matured and learned from those days in the glade? What if I have the right views now?"

I look back down at the man in the water, he doesn't look angry, his face is one of cold calculation, like he thinks it was a fair question that deserves to be addressed. "Well, allow me to answer

130

your question through a series of some of my own," he says. "Peri, what do you want most?"

I think about the question, knowing that it is deeper than it seemed. After a moment I come up with a few items I felt confident were the truest answers. "Life, happiness, and security."

"For yourself?" the man asks.

"Of course," I say, "and for anybody else brave enough to seek them. I think they deserve those things."

"Alright then," the man says, "now allow me to compare to you two worlds, the glade and your now passed land. In one you had life and happiness, but you didn't care about your security, you took life as it came. In the other, you had security, but were you happy? And did you really have life?"

"Of course I had life, I had more than I had ever experienced before! For the first time I could control the life taken."

"And yet for all that," the man says, "can you really say it was living? You were always concerned about something or other. You were never relaxed or truly happy, you merely moved from one project to another. Look at these walls Peri. You grew up with these walls, and you always wanted to get out of them, so why do you create your own now?"

I am about to reply to the man in the water, give him a well deserved education on just who he is in relation to me, just how little he matters with his small minds and little dreams. I open my mouth and raise my finger, already planning the speech to be produced, when I blink, and it all disappears.

Just like that, all sign of my childhood is gone again. I sit there frozen, processing just what happened, still holding my mouth open in the air now empty but for the stars swirling where blue light once glowed. As I sit there I feel sudden embarrassment, but more than that, I feel shame. I had accepted that the man in the water only wanted to help me, I had told myself that I had been the problem, I had even nearly apologized for all I had done, and still I had been riled by my pride to destroy any minuscule shred of friendship that could possibly still exist between the two of us.

I make a promise then as I stand up on the mountain. I look up and see that the yellow light is closer now, I can see now that it is far larger than I originally thought. I look at the light and speak out my promise into the starry air, they will serve as my witnesses. "If I ever see the man in the water again, I promise I will do everything in my power or whatever power really does rule the worlds to reconcile. I promise I'll apologize and take the blame for the problems we have faced. And most of all promise I won't let my pride get in the way of things this time. And if it's Disha I manage to meet again, then I will do all of this for her as well. I don't yet know how I'll do it, but I must change my life, before life is no longer mine."

And with that thought, I turn to my left and began again walking forward up the path that slopes up and now around the mountain. I feel I had a decent grip on just how this mountain works now. Soon I will come across the island as I had the valley and the glade. I pray that there I will meet Disha. I;m confident this would be the chance for me to turn it all around, so I continue to walk forward.

XIX

As I walk the path becomes rougher, rocks jutting out of the ground and lining the path so that it becomes perilous to step down for fear that the stone beneath my foot is sharp or loose, causing it to roll away and make me fall down. In addition, many of the stars have collected on the floor of the mountain path, making the small bits of solid ground slippery and appear deceitfully smooth. I cut and bruise my arms and legs as I continue on, but still I march forward, determined to come to the island and find Disha.

I try blinking often as I walk, hoping that this might trigger the appearance of Disha, but it seems to do nothing to prompt this event. I walk for hours and begin feeling angry. Here I am, trying to actually get my life back together, trying to reconcile my relationships with the people that always seem to pop into my life when I least want them to. But now, when I want to do the right thing, they are nowhere to be found. I hope this doesn't mean that they have left me for good, leaving me to my own miseries as I probably deserve. I feel on the edge of tears of frustration. What am I supposed to do?

Wrapped in my thoughts I barely notice the path suddenly slanting down at a concerning angle to fall a good thirty feet downwards. Before I even register what this means I am sliding down the incline at an alarming rate. I spin and fall over rocks hidden below the stars, I feel an immense pain in my shoulder as my arm is jerked when I fall on it at the bottom of the slope.

I sit at the bottom of the path, trying not to pass out or go into shock from the cascading waves of pain emanating out of my shoulder. I look over at it and nearly throw up as I see the angle my arm sit at, it is so grotesque and abnormal. The pain is nearly unbearable, but I manage to sit up and assess the damage. Any attempts to move my bad arm result in my nearly blacking out from the pain it causes. I can see what has to be done to restore my arm, but the knowledge doesn't provide any comfort.

I take my good hand and hold it over the top of the arm. I count to ten, trying to suppress my panic and build my courage, then grab the shoulder and pulled it back into the socket as quickly as I can. The feeling is indescribable, first a furious burning that feels about to overwhelm me like the eruption I survived when I was younger, only this is much, much worse, then after the burning there is a feeling of relief like a river of ice water coming in to sooth burns. It's like a mounting tension I couldn't even feel until it's gone. My arm is still sore, but the main pain has dissipated.

I sit there in the stars, resting a moment before standing in the cold air. Looking up at the slope I had fallen from I'm a little surprised to see just how gentle it is, at least compared to some of the other risks I had overcome in days past. I give a rue smile and have to accept the hard truth that I'm simply not as young or able as I once had been. Gone were the days when I might fall from mountains and leave unscathed, now tripping on a rock could be fatal.

I begin walking forward, temporarily forgetting about finding the man in the water or Disha while considering my current state. Coming around a corner though, I instantly remember where I am. Scattered along the ground here and coming out of the walls are dozens of stone arms reaching out to grab anyone near enough to fall prey to their hands. I've nearly forgotten about these, the hands of the Extranos that had chased me into the glade in the dark tunnel.

In that darkness I hadn't known what was going on, didn't know that danger was all around, but still I feared what I did not know. My ignorant fear had proven well founded, since the Extranos had tried to kill me in that tunnel before I could make it out safely. I look at the arms now, wilding flailing around and grasping at the stars moving in the air. They seem to be aligned in a circular pattern converging around a central point where there seems to be a refuge from the hands.

I walk up to the outer edge of the ring, not knowing where else to go, and as I near the hands moved aside so at to let me pass. It may be a trap of some kind, them trying to lure me in beyond the point where I can escape, but I walk forward anyway.

The hands continue clearing away as I advance, making a clear path of sorts for me. I continue walking until I am in the center point of the circle, and sigh in resignation. There, maybe two feet in diameter, is a circle of death. It is the only death I have seen the whole way up this mountain, and it isn't without its victims. All around the circle of death, there is a faint glowing, a pink light framing the hole like a sad halo.

Its meaning is all too clear to me as I look on, surrounded by the stars drifting in the air. This glow, this death, could only be the final resting place of one of my only friends. Disha, has died.

Standing there, I feel no misting of my eyes or constriction in my throat. I do not feel an overwhelming sadness or emptiness as I come to the realization that Disha is indeed dead. No, I feel only cold looking at the haloed circle burned into the dirt like a brand against skin. *Perhaps I'm in shock,* I think, *perhaps it will hit me later on.* But I don't believe it, I feel confident I will never truly feel sadness at this passing.

It's not because I'm cruel or heartless that I feel this way, but rather because the emotion that clouds my mind and pushes out my sadness is one of furious anger. I have not killed Disha, but I will never know what did. I pushed her away, I rejected her counsel and I made her leave my world, which caused the excommunication of us two. I couldn't be the person she wanted me to be, I could not be selfless or see beyond my nose for so long that I have forever lost my chance. I will now never be able to apologize to the girl who fought for me when I wouldn't. I would now never be able to thank her.

Because she is gone, and likely enough I will soon be in the same state. I kneel down next to the sort of grave and trace my finger all around the pink ring, adding a blue one to mix in and produce a purple color. As I do the hands disappear back into the floor, and I use this opportunity to write more on the ground there.

Peri

Here rests Disha, a girl of the registana
She was brave, selfless, and kind
She never let a friend fall without jumping after
She always knew the truth and the best way to see it
Wherever she has now traveled, she is surely peaceful
Because she deserved peace more than anyone

After writing my small message, I sign my name at the bottom. I may have rejected her while she lived, but if I can't rewrite the past I'll try to claim her now, making amends as best I can. Once I have signed the epitaph the wind picks up and the stars spin around my head like restless birds. I watch the short note, expecting it to soon turn into paper and fly away into the sky to be read by whomever follows me, but this does not happen. Instead, as I watch the words through the swirling stars I see these same stars begin running into the blue light, charging forward directly into the ground.

Millions of these stars must pound into the floor until finally the wind dies down and the stars finally return to their gentle dances. The words however, don't return to normal. The stars have somehow gone *into* the letters on the ground so that they now seemed to delve into the mountain for miles. Before it looked like a flat blue light reaching into the air, now it looks as though each word is a tunnel into the stone, where the stars make up the walls. If one moves one's head the letters appear to sparkle and glitter from thousands upon thousands of points of lights. I'm astounded, but also grateful, satisfied. This is the kind of gift Disha deserves, and it is one, I can admit, that I could not give her.

I stand from the spot, knowing that my time to move on has come. I can't remain here in the dark forever, one has to move back into the light, moving on with the life one has been given here and now, while it was still in one's possession. I walk forward on the path, not focusing on the things I had lost for the first time in my life. I am truly moving on, and this time, I fully intend to not look back.

I walk on, wondering what this mountain will bring to me next, keeping in mind just how close the yellow light above me is getting. It's still far off, but its imminence is clearly evident as I continue advancing up this slope. As I walk the ground again changes. The stars are thicker here both on the ground and in the air, causing my footfalls to make only soft crunching noises and my vision to be obstructed more than ever. I can hardly see anything when my foot suddenly steps into a puddle of water up to my calf and the temperature rises to boiling.

The stars continue drifting in the air, oblivious to the sweltering warmth, but they clear enough for me to get a bearing and discover just where I am. As I expected I've come to a likeness of the island, though Disha will not be meeting me here as I hoped. I look down at my wet leg and see that I had stepped not in a puddle as I had thought, but rather in the very ocean I once considered vast and untraversable. I step from the warm water and stand on the sandy mainland of the island.

Strangely though, I notice the sand here is not made of the death the island's had been formed of, being composed instead of the dark stone that made up the walls and Extranos, maintaining the pattern of no death on this mountain with the exception of Disha's grave. Where all the death here is held I do not know, or perhaps there simply is any. Maybe this world is without death, the only such world that actually exists. But even if this is true, it does have its weak points such as the circular grave. Perhaps the death has pockets where it hides waiting for unsuspecting wanderers hoping to snatch them up when they've let down their guard. In my experience with the death, this is plausible, but even so I don't fear the possibility. If I die now, I die. Really what more is there to live for?

As soon as I think it, I immediately dispel the thought and curse myself for giving up so easily. Death won't succeed over me so easily, of that I am still determined. The source of my determination lay not in my sense of self preservation or pride as it once had, but rather from the tenacious conviction that I must try my very best to meet the man in the water one last time. I must reconcile with him as I hadn't been able to with Disha. Perhaps I will die before I get the chance, but it won't be because I accept my fate without a fight. That has never been my way, and I don't intend to start giving up now.

I look down on the little mountain in the center of this miniature island, no more than a molehill framed against the monstrous peak it stands on, and I consider how much time I wasted trying to climb it.

Looking at how little it is in reality, I wonder just how important it ever was that I climb it. Had it really had the effect I'd been so sure it would? How much could it have changed when in the grand scheme of my life it had been only a short moment, a minor event. It made me wonder what other parts of my life I placed such importance on when they were no more than molehills on mountains.

I run my hands through the stone sand on the ground, bringing a blue glow into the sifting sediment. The effect is beautiful. Everywhere I touch the sand glows blue, but all the other sand still keeps its dull, lackluster, dark hue, making swirling patterns of color and light in seas of normality and darkness. I watch these swirls move as I continue passing my hands into them, watching life enter the dead stone. I remember how Disha and I had first fallen onto the island, falling onto the death sand at the same point where I now trace my fingers.

The water had been all around me, keeping me on the land where I could see no way out, but there was the mountain. There had always been the mountain on that island, taunting me, daring me to try and climb it, making me question what could possibly be at the top of such a dauntless peak. I never knew what I would find, but I was always determined to try and see just what was held at the very top. Nearly the entire time I had lived on that island I pushed myself, through every struggle, to just make it to the top. I had wanted to be able to look out at the island and say that I had made it there myself, through hard work and dedication and a simple desire to just make it once in my life.

I'd been pushed around in the glade, a slave to the whims of fate and destiny, but when I got to the island I decided that my fate was in my hands, and that success is accomplished only through a determination to put in the extra work, even when it hurts, even when you don't know what success even means for sure, you just keep trying. That had always been my motivation when I was wondering where to go, what to do, how long to stay on that island.

And then, after time and effort, Disha and I made the effort to climb the mountain. The trip seemed easy, everything was going our way, the ground was even moving us upwards so we could sit back and relax, just coast our way to the top of the peak. At least, that's what we thought. We had seemed so close to the top, it would be only a very short time until I could stand at my peak as I had dreamed since arriving, I grew complacent. I didn't look two feet ahead because I was too busy looking to the top.

And so I had fallen.

I suppose I should have paid attention then, taking that humbling event to heart and remember that arrogance does not buy steps up a mountain. One doesn't advance to the top by growing lazy or cocky, the world didn't owe me a chance at getting to the top as I had once thought, if I wanted something I had to put in the time and work. It had been my initial belief, but I had lost it, and that was why I had fallen and nearly shattered my leg, crippling me for my next attempt.

Yet, though I was hurt and I failed, I was still determined to get to the top of that mountain. I'm ashamed looking at the little mountain now, remembering just how I went about things. I had been creative and determined, but not for the right reasons. It wasn't about getting to the top to have some claim of ownership. It wasn't to find some glorious thing at the top of the peak. It wasn't even to try and escape the island. No, the real reason I had wanted so badly to get to the top the second time was simply to prove to the mountain that I could. I wanted to show that lifeless but cruel edifice that I was the master of my fate, and that I wouldn't be cheated by something so insignificant as itself.

So I made tools, I rested and healed as best I could, I made plans. The mountain thought that giving me a bad leg would spare it from my determined quest, but I would prove to it that it could not injure me, that I would come again, and again, and agin, until I stood on its peak and showed truly who was in control between us two.

It's embarrassing to remember the pride, the ignorance and outright conceit I possessed at that time. What had once been a noble pursuit of knowledge and desire to better myself became a corrupt, ravenous hunger for control and ownership. I thought I was so much more than everything around me. I was a molehill on my own mountain, as insignificant in reality as this scale island on my path.

I don't wait this time for the world to disappear, I blink and am back to the mountain's true path. It's a time I was embarrassed about, but I don't need to dwell on it any longer to appreciate how low I fell. I try to learn my lesson and move on. This is what I do with my life now, I try to move on, and I continue now.

I was almost afraid of seeing the next chapter of my life, knowing that it was the darkest stain on the black fabric that is my life. I made mistakes, I did horrible, selfish things, and there is no doubt that these things took refuge in that next chapter, thriving in the environment I provided them with plenty of food and water to grow.

For the next section of my life was when I rejected my friends, my dreams, and my hope of finding a better life. Instead I decided to craft my own, not out of ambition or a hope to do good, but rather out of my insatiable need for control and ownership. I wanted to be the one to call the shots, I wanted to be the one to change the rules, and I wanted to be the one that burned others rather than getting burned myself.

I walk on and saw it only a little ways ahead, blinking doesn't bring this one on, this place has been here the entire time, marking its existence on the mountain, refusing to be ignored. It is waiting for me.

XX

There are mountains, the river running freely where it would, the hills existing at random, trees scattered here and there. As I draw closer the mountains melt and reform, creating archways, six gates at equal intervals. The hills coalesce into the larger mound in the center, a ring of water forming around it. The trees move to their appropriate forests, the paths cutting straight through each of them. Lastly, a throne erects in the center of the hill, waiting for its occupant.

This is not a world with secrets to discover, a world that is alive and baits the curious to go explore. This is not the kind of world where one can wander around for hours, looking for hiding places from imaginary enemies. This is not the sort of world where I would draw on walls, filling the land with a magical blue glow fueled by dreaming up impossible creatures. No, this world is not like that, this world was dead from the moment I stepped into it, and for all my efforts of defeating death I merely created a land where it was right at home.

I look down at the diagram of sorts displaying the domain I had once been so proud to claim as my own and I notice something strange. Where my stone trees had been, including the large one behind my throne, there are only normal trees, none of the actual stone sentinels are to be found here. Though it's odd I'm grateful for this fact, I don't want more salt in my wounds reminding me of all the harm I've caused, both to the bit of land that was my own to claim, at least in my own mind, and to myself and the relationships I kept and lost.

But even as I watch these small trees, out of the ground stalks shoot up and with a sigh I recognize that these are the stone trees. As I watch I see the blue handprints appear on each of the trunks, my little brand on my little world, trying to pretend that it was a universe and I was its god. And so the arrogance of man in its largest scope is brought into the light when shown just how small its claim is.

After a while I see many of the Extranos wandering around the little land, doing their different jobs and occasionally yelling out or working with a piece of land or stone. There's something distinctly different about these Extranos though, and I can't understand it. These stone men aren't made of stone.

There's no doubt in my mind that these are indeed Extranos as their identity is clearly displayed by the tasks they perform and their way of walking without much purpose. Even with this being the case though, where I had always seen their skin to be a dark grey color, marked by my brand on each and every one of their heads, now they all have real skin and clothing. Some have skin tones of deep brown or lighter tans, some shades of white or red, some are men and some women. It's insane, I know that these people had been made of simple, indistinguishable stone, and now they have real flesh and blood, and clothing ranging from the elegant to the bland.

Here I can see countless real people, people with stories I don't know, could never know now. Each one of these people is lost to me now forever just like Disha, and possibly the man in the water as well. I feel bad about this for some reason, like I've somehow wronged these people by not knowing their true nature. I wish I could now speak with just one of these people, to truly know who they are, and how they're real when they had always appeared so inauthentic.

"Um, I believe you wanted to speak with me master?" An unfamiliar voice asks behind me. My eyes burst wide and I spin around to see one of the men I had seen below me is now here, in the flesh, which is indeed very different from the stone. My mouth drops open and I struggle for words.

"H-how did you... When did... What?" I stutter.

"I'm not quite sure how I got here master, but you needed me for something?" the man in front of me asks.

I'm very confused, but I'm not going to waste this opportunity, not when I'm finally getting past that. "Um, yes, I guess, maybe I did, I don't know. Are you, that is to say, were you one of the Extranos?"

"You did call us that master, back in the deathless lands."

"Not so deathless in the end, eh?" I mutter with a smile that holds no humor. "Do um, do you have a name?"

"They call me Maluum master," he says.

"Please, Maluum, stop calling me master. I'm not your master. I never was. Just one feeble person pretending to be more than was true."

Maluum seems confused, his brow furrowing. "Well then, what do I call you?" he asks.

I walk over to him, put my hand on his shoulder, look him in the eye and say, "Peri. You can all me Peri, Maluum. It's my name, it's who I am."

Maluum looks very uncomfortable, "But, Master, I can't call you by your name," he protest, "it isn't appropriate. I'm just a servant, no one special, you are my ruler."

I chuckle wryly, "A ruler of what, Maluum? Look around you, is this my country? No, the only land I ever ruled is sitting at your feet, hardly reaching up to your knee. That's the thing about kingdoms on earth, Maluum, they grow, and they disappear. Nothing lasts forever in a finite world."

"But your kingdom will come again! It didn't fade away, it was destroyed," he says, "by that man and woman that came in, the country was fine till they came. Everything you had built was torn down by them, it would have lasted forever."

"A fairly weak empire that can be torn down by two unarmed people, wouldn't you say?" I reply, hearing in Maluum's arguments my own. "They destroyed nothing more than the illusion of something. There never was a real kingdom, never any kind of land that I truly ruled. I was nothing more than a puppet of fate, used as an instrument but nothing more. They destroyed nothing because there was nothing to destroy."

Maluum still looks confused, maybe even frustrated, but he doesn't protest again. All he says is, "If you say so...Peri."

"I do Maluum, thank you for understanding." I look around the mountain where we stand. I don't exactly know what to do with Maluum. Am I supposed to take him with me to the peak? Looking up I see it is beginning to get tantalizingly close, but even still it will be a hard journey, and I don't know what is on the top. The last time

I had taken someone up a mountain I thought I lost them forever. No, I don't know why Maluum is here exactly, but I'm not meant to take him with me.

"Maluum," I say, "why don't we sit down?" We both sit on the hard ground, avoiding the center piece of my domain surrounding my mock throne. "So Maluum, tell me about yourself. I'm actually very interested in your life." Maluum still doesn't look comfortable, as though this is all a trap to get him into trouble. "Please," I say, trying to reassure him, "this isn't an examination, nothing you say is going to put you at risk. I'm just curious. If you don't want to answer you don't have to, nothing is going to happen to you, I promise."

As I say the last words I remember the last promise I made to the Extranos, my promise they wouldn't die. I have to make up for my lie. I have to keep this promise.

Maluum still looks uncertain but he asks, "Well Peri, where exactly do you want me to start?"

I smile, "How about the beginning, Maluum? That seems like a good opening."

I can see the smallest hint of a smile climb up one side of Maluum's face, "I suppose so. Well, I don't quite know where the beginning was, but I remember a long time ago, as far back as I can remember in fact, I lived in this awful place. The walls, they were so very high, and dark. You know how the sun was always low in your world?" I nod, "Well where I once lived the sun couldn't even be seen. Here you have stars, there it was just always gray, depressing, dead.

"There was always a lot of death, sometimes so deep you could fall in just by walking over it. I saw people do that a lot back then, just die because they could never get out of that pit. Other people, they didn't die, they just forgot what light was. See, not everyone was born into that world like I was, some had fallen into the pit on accident. They knew what the sun was, but they forgot that it mattered. They accepted the darkness and despair that the pit offered.

"There was no way out of that pit, no way to escape from the death on the ground or the darkness in the air. It wasn't just a physical place, it was a frame of mind. The pit could only really hold you if you let it."

"I see what you mean," I say quietly. "The heaviest chains are the ones we use to shackle our minds."

"Exactly!" Maluum exclaims, getting excited and displaying a light in his eyes. "That's how I always felt about it, but some of them just couldn't see the possibility that there may be a way out of the pit. They accepted their fates like they had no control over them. Nothing like you, you always took your life into your own hands!"

Though it's meant as a compliment the phrase causes me to feel only shame. "Well," I say, "that may be true Maluum, but I don't think it was always for the best reasons."

"Well, at least you tried!" Maluum says, "They would just sit around, complaining about how bad things were but never actually doing anything to improve their lives. I never understood how people that were so dissatisfied with their lives could never make even the slightest attempt to change it. They were so unwilling to take risks, either because they had once and failed, or because they just couldn't see the light enough to know the point.

"But then we started hearing about someone far away, someone who was creating a world without death. This person cared about the people like us that didn't matter. This person opened the borders of that land so we could come in and live so much better than we were before. Most of us were intrigued, but hardly anybody cared enough to try and get to this land. But I cared, and I was sure I would get to that land, even if I was the only one."

I remain silent as Maluum speaks, knowing that he's talking about me and my land, but also knowing that he has romanticized a selfish, uncaring person. They believed the lies I told. I believed the lies I told. In the end though, they are still just lies. "Maluum, you should know…" I start.

"Please, let me finish," Maluum says, cringing, as though he expects me to grow angry with him for interrupting me.

"Oh," I say, realizing he is waiting for permission, "of course, go ahead."

"You see," he continues, "I finally did get out of that pit. I saw an opportunity, a light, for the first time in my life. I didn't have a ladder or a flight of stairs, there wasn't any easy way to get up above the walls to where the world rested, so I made pick and climbed the whole way up to the top. Many people told me it was stupid, to give up on and just accept my status as permanent, but I ignored them and made it to the top. After that it was a short journey to your world, I just sort of appeared there."

"When I did arrive, I saw hundreds of people who like me had made it to a new opportunity. I felt like I had finally accomplished something in my life. I had risen out of the pit I had so long lived in and found a new world, a world with the sun on my face and hope to be found. It was like I had finally found a home."

I remembered how I felt much the same when I created the hill and mountains, molding the land to my taste. I had felt like I had escaped from the life of being controlled into making my fate my own. I can relate to what Maluum is saying, and yet, he had had it so much harder than I ever had. In retrospect my life had always been so easy. Did I have any right to complain?

That's the tricky thing about unhappiness. Somebody has had it worse than you did. There's always some place in the world where your most basic commodities were luxurious indulgences. Does this mean you have no right to feel unhappy or dissatisfied? No, I decide, that's not what it means at all. If I hadn't yearned for something more in my own life, in the same way that Maluum had, then the things Maluum had wanted would never have been accomplished. For all I know he's able to do even greater things in his life than I ever had or would. Perhaps us all coming from different areas in life, all experiences with different levels of pain and equating them as the same allowed us all to collectively move forward into that world where death truly did not exist, where we can banish our pain as easily as blowing dust from a ledge.

I wait to see if Maluum has anything else to add, and when silence is my answer I clear my throat and say, "Maluum, there's some things you should know, about me." Maluum sits up and looks attentive. "You see, I, I'm not the hero you make me out to be. I didn't make my world in an attempt to help people, I didn't allow you all to live there so that you could escape death or reach your dreams."

"I don't know what you mean," Maluum says, "what other purpose could it have served, it was a haven for the cheated in life."

"Even if that were true," I say, "though it's not, the only 'cheated' I had in mind to protect and provide a home for was myself. See, in the same way you always felt held in by the walls of that pit, the way that you wanted to see the sun, I wanted to control the sun. I wanted to control my life, the same as you, but I wanted to do it because I wanted authority, I wanted power. I wanted people, slaves, under me so that I could feel like their god and have them serve me or face death. I wanted life and death to be in my hands. Even the sun obeyed my commands then, and I thought that made me special."

Maluum raises an eyebrow, "But, there's nothing wrong with that. We all want control, you were simply strong enough to take it. That's something worthy of respect, not disdain."

I smile and look at my feet. "Ya know Maluum" I say, "I once thought the same thing. I thought other people were beneath me because they didn't have my vision or strength, but in reality, I was just a weak willed soul who could never appreciate the things I had because I always wanted more. That's not strength Maluum, that's immaturity."

"But..." Maluum starts, but he seems so confused it's causing him pain. He doesn't say anything for a few moments. He just looks at me, expecting me to somehow have his answer. I can't blame him, I had trained this man that the sun rose and set on me, that I am the beginning and the end of all life and order. Who else would he look to for his answers?

"Maluum, I'm sorry," I say rising from my spot and walking over to him. "I used you and the others under me. I was selfish uncaring towards you all, which you neither deserved nor should have been expected to simply maintain. I'm glad if I can inspire you to reach for more for your life, because please don't misunderstand, ambition is not wrong. You, my friend, deserve to reach for every one of these stars in this sky, and I believe you could actually get to them. But, I have still wronged you, and so I apologize for that.

"I'd like you to make a promise, but only if you want to, you don't have to do this. Will you promise to forgive me for my horrible treatment of you, and to do something greater with your life than settle for petty power or control. You can reach the full potential I missed Maluum, just try not to fall into the groove I cut in the path. Can you do that?"

Maluum doesn't answer for a moment, obviously very conflicted about this decision, then he looks me in the eye and says, "Well, Peri, I can try."

I smile at this man. A man I still don't know very well, but by now I feel I understand him well. I pull him into an embrace, and hold him there until he, and the hills, arches, rivers, and trees of the land fade back into the solid stone of the mountain. Then, I turn around, and walk up, preparing for the end of my journey.

XXI

I look up at the yellow glow. Now the light has an evident source, though I still can't tell just what that is. It's like there is a shape made of a yellow so bright it is pure white, and it cut into the dark night air as easily as I can separate the death in the ground. I can't see where the white stops and the yellow starts, but the outer ends of the glow reaching the farthest into the night do give off a brilliant golden glow.

I look at it, still from a distance but so close I feel sure I will reach it in only an hour or two. The light of this mysterious object leaves me in awe, speechless at the beauty and magnificence the light possesses, the perfect way it captures beauty in such a pure, clean way. I think about when I controlled the sun, how the light had been at my command then. I thought I could make it do whatever I wanted, but I know that even with a million suns I could never make anything half so stunning as this object of light. As I draw nearer I'm possessed in having to know what this thing could be.

I feel sure if I learn this then everything about this mountain will make sense. Why am I here, and how have I gotten here? Where is here anyway? Why do I keep seeing these scenes from my past, and when will the journey be over? I can guess the answer to the last question is when I reach the light at the top of the mountain, but the last time I climbed a mountain it had resulted in only finding another world. Who can say whether that won't happen again.

As much as I want to see that light though, to reach its glory, there is still one more person I want the chance to speak with before I come to the peak. I had seen the man in the water once since I had started on this mountain, and I had messed up the discussion beyond repair. Disha had passed away before I could ever apologize to her, and if I don't get the chance to do so with the man in the water I know it will hold me down forever, allowing me no pleasure or comfort for the rest of eternity. I hope that not everything that has happened on this mountain is so permanent that I don't get another chance with the man. Whatever it takes, I want to speak with him just once more.

The path takes a sharp turn here, opening into a cul-de-sac with the walls only about eight feet high. How this place has existed without my seeing any sign of it till now I don't know, for lining the walls on every visible space was every drawing or note I had ever etched along the walls. The amount of blue glowing light that emanates from these walls is nearly blinding, and I have to raise my arm over my eyes to protect them from the onslaught of light ahead of me. And yet, I am in love with this place.

In one small corner there is this entire account of my life through the things I have drawn and written. If I look closely I can see some of the individual pictures or words. There are the mushrooms I had drawn, here is a short essay written when I was a child about the nature of the death. A little ways off there is a handprint probably marking some berry bush or hiding spot. I look on and nearly cry at how much history is held on these walls, but then, even as I watch the glow begins to fade and the etchings disappear from before me. I cry out and run to the walls, but don't touch them for fear of covering up the things already marked down and fading away. I fall on the ground as everything fades away, feeling like my life is being taken away without a trace, as though it has no place here any longer.

Soon enough the walls are clean from any light. Only the dark gray stone remains as the stars drift through the air from above. I sit there, mourning the loss of things passed, when I have an idea. I may not be able to keep my past in my pocket, I may not be able to look back on it at all times, but I can give the account myself.

I stand and walk as far to the left of this cul-de-sac as I can and begin writing. I start with my awakening in that cave and continue. I write about my dig through death to start my life. I write about the valley where I first saw death, where I learned to fear it. I write about the man in the water that became my friend. I write about the forests that were so vast that I got lost in them, seeming only to repeat my life and its common difficulties again and again until finally I managed to learn from my mistakes and leave that part of my life. I write about the dark tunnel, the glade, the island and its mountain, and I write about the domain I shaped.

I take special care to give instruction throughout this particularly lengthy note. I want it to be clear to anyone reading that I had been so mistaken in my view of the world and the way I climbed the mountain that was my life. I had started with a desire to do such good, I just wanted to learn and discover, to create, understand, and play. My friends were so important to me once, I would do anything for them. But somewhere in my life I had changed from that desire that to wanting those same friends to do things for me, to be the slaves to the dream I never let fall away. I write about how I used the Extranos, seeing them so little that I didn't even realize they were people just like me, how I was able to see past them into what they could do for me.

I write about how I then rejected my friends, Disha and the man in the water. How they had come to me to help me and stop me from the destructive path they saw that I was on and I had cast them out, ignored their counsel and had to watch my world rot before me. I write about just how temporary our paper kingdoms are, how one stiff breeze or heavy rain can topple them in an instant.

I also write about my eternity of mourning, my rejection of the past life I had suffered before I woke into a world of stars, both above and below. I write about how this repentance had been wasted when I met again with he man in the water and done more harm than before, how I may have lost him forever. I write about how Disha died and I hadn't been able to truly say goodbye. I write about the one Extrano I had ever truly met, my friend Maluum, and how I tried to convince that though he had a different image of me, I had been wrong all this time.

I write about how I came into this nook on the mountain, how I saw my past fade before my eyes, and how I preserved it in a different manner. I write and write and write until every wall in this nook is completely covered, bathing the reader in the glowing mark I leave on the world. When I have finally written everything there is to write I take a step back, and look at all I have written, all I have lived.

There are chapters I am proud of, and some that bring me only shame. Regardless though, this is me, and though there was pain, there was also life. Standing there at the end I let out a breath and for the first time am content with the world.

"One thing left to do," a voice says. Turning I see the man is waiting for me next to a doorway of sorts. The golden-white light emanates from within, shining out into the star laden night.

I look in the eyes of the man, the only one who had been with me since the beginning, and I can see that there are no words left to say. I repent, and he forgives. Now, I need only join him for this one, last journey.

I take a few shuffling steps forward, finding that my feet have lost their past grace and strength. I take the man's outstretched hand in my own and we both turn to face the doorway. There are no marks that need to be made, no death to fear. For the first time in my life, I recognize that passing on isn't truly dying, it is living.

With this thought in my mind and the man's fingers in my hand, I take a step forward and am surrounded by light.

Acknowledgements

There are few things in this world that we can do alone if we want to do them well. Books have never been an exception to this rule. Though the task of writer can be given only to one (at least in this case) there are yet those without whom I honestly believe this book would never have been written or printed.

Primarily I would like to thank my God, who has blessed me with the education and opportunity to make this book a reality. As the great composer Johann Sebastian Bach wrote on all of his music, Soli Deo Gloria. To God be the Glory alone.

I would also like to thank my family. My parents and siblings have always been very supportive of my writing, encouraging me to write more and reading many of my stories (which is a true sacrifice I don't doubt). They are the ones who first pushed me to continue writing and pursue my dreams.

Next I would like to thank Miss. Tiffany Rott, a fellow author and friend who was a constant springboard for any ideas I wanted to bounce off of her during the writing period of this book. I'm sure she grew quite tired of hearing about shifting worlds and stone men, but she humored me and kept me on track with my writing, while also being willing to edit.

I'd also like to thank my mentor in many areas, Patrick Kavanaugh, who gave me a practical ambitious drive. He taught me to not only to want something, but to actually make that desire happen with planning and organization. His guidance was invaluable.

There are a number of authors whom I grew up knowing, Samuel Schiller, Richard Bradford, David M. Daniels, Vickie Peach Wilkins, Suzanne Gose, and more. They all encouraged me to write and showed me a tangible example of how my dream was attainable. Their example is one I hope I can emulate one day to other writers.

I have also had countless supporters in the form of readers. Every story that I finished they would read and critique, giving me a passion to write more. In many ways this book is for them, my friends, mentors, and confidants. They are the ones who asked for a book, and so one was written.

I offer a thank you truly too large for words to every man and woman who works in the tea industry. Your dedication and work has been much appreciated over the course of writing this book.

Lastly I would sincerely like to thank *you*, reader. Cliche as you may think it I am in earnest. I believe firmly that books don't belong to their writers, but to their readers. It is your task to discover a world and explore it. You fill in the colors and details. You paint your own picture of the characters and the world they inhabit. *You* finished this book. Without your imagination it would be a far shallower text, and so I thank you for your service to this little book.